VIRGINIA SLAVE NARRATIVES

A Folk History of Slavery in Virginia
from Interviews with Former Slaves

* * *

Typewritten records prepared by
THE FEDERAL WRITERS' PROJECT
1936-1938

* * *

Published in cooperation with
THE LIBRARY OF CONGRESS

APPLEWOOD BOOKS
Bedford, Massachusetts

The LIBRARY
of CONGRESS

A portion of the proceeds from the sale
of this book is donated to the Library of
Congress, which holds the original Slave
Narratives in its collection.

Thank you for purchasing an Applewood book.
Applewood reprints America's lively classics
--books from the past that are still of
interest to modern readers. For a free copy
of our current catalog, write to:

Applewood Books
P.O. Box 365
Bedford, MA 01730

ISBN 1-55709-025-4

FOREWORD

More than 140 years have elapsed since the ratification of the Thirteenth Amendment to the U.S. Constitution declared slavery illegal in the United States, yet America is still wrestling with the legacy of slavery. One way to examine and understand the legacy of the 19th Century's "peculiar institution" in the 21st century is to read and listen to the stories of those who actually lived as slaves. It is through a close reading of these personal narratives that Americans can widen their understanding of the past, thus enriching the common memory we share.

The American Folklife Center at the Library of Congress is fortunate to hold a powerful and priceless sampling of sound recordings, manuscript interviews, and photographs of former slaves. The recordings of former slaves were made in the 1930s and early 1940s by folklorists John A. and Ruby T. Lomax, Alan Lomax, Zora Neale Hurston, Mary Elizabeth Barnicle, John Henry Faulk, Roscoe Lews, and others. These aural accounts provide the only existing sound of voices from the institution of slavery by individuals who had been held in bondage three generations earlier. These voices can be heard by visiting the web site http://memory.loc.gov/ammem/collections/voices/. Added to the Folklife Center collections, many of the narratives from manuscript sources, which you find in this volume, were collected under the auspices of the United States Works Progress Administration (WPA), and were known as the slave narrative collection. These transcripts are found in the Library of Congress Manuscript Division. Finally, in addition to the Folklife Center photographs, a treasure trove of Farm Security Administration (FSA) photographs (including those of many former slaves) reside in the Prints and Photographs Division here at the nation's library. Together, these primary source materials on audio tape, manuscript and photographic formats are a unique research collection for all who would wish to study and understand the emotions, nightmares, dreams, and determination of former slaves in the United States.

The slave narrative sound recordings, manuscript materials, and photographs are invaluable as windows through which we can observe and be touched by the experiences of slaves who lived in the mid-19th century. At the same time, these archival materials are the fruits of an extraordinary documentary effort of the 1930s. The federal government, as part of its response to the Great Depression, organized unprecedented national initiatives to document the lives, experiences, and cultural traditions of ordinary Americans. The slave narratives, as documents of the Federal Writers Project, established and delineated our modern concept of "oral history." Oral history, made possible by the advent of sound recording technology, was "invented" by folklorists, writers, and other cultural documentarians under the aegis of the Library of Congress and various WPA offices—especially the Federal Writers' project—during the 1930s. Oral history has subsequently become both a new tool for the discipline of history, and a new cultural pastime undertaken in homes, schools, and communities by Americans of all walks of life. The slave narratives you read in the pages that follow stand as our first national exploration of the idea of oral history, and the first time that ordinary Americans were made part of the historical record.

The American Folklife Center has expanded upon the WPA tradition by continuing to collect oral histories from ordinary Americans. Contemporary projects such as our Veterans History Project, StoryCorps Project, Voices of Civil Rights Project, as well as our work to capture the stories of Americans after September 11, 2001 and of the survivors of Hurricanes Katrina and Rita, are all adding to the Library of Congress holdings that will enrich the history books of the future. They are the oral histories of the 21st century.

Frederick Douglas once asked: can "the white and colored people of this country be blended into a common nationality, and enjoy together...under the same flag, the inestimable blessings of life, liberty, and the pursuit of happiness, as neighborly citizens of a common country? I believe they can." We hope that the words of the former slaves in these editions from Applewood Books will help Americans achieve Frederick Douglas's vision of America by enlarging our understanding of the legacy of slavery in all of our lives. At the same time, we in the American Folklife Center and the Library of Congress hope these books will help readers understand the importance of oral history in documenting American life and culture—giving a voice to all as we create our common history.

Peggy A. Bulger

Peggy Bulger
Director, The American Folklife Center
Library of Congress

A NOTE FROM THE PUBLISHER

Since 1976, Applewood Books has been republishing books from America's past. Our mission is to build a picture of America through its primary sources. The book you hold in your hand is a testament to that mission. Published in cooperation with the Library of Congress, this collection of slave narratives is reproduced exactly as writers in the Works Progress Administration's Federal Writers' Project (1936–1938) originally typed them.

As publishers, we thought about how to present these documents. Rather than making them more readable by resetting the type, we felt that there was more value in presenting the narratives in their original form. We believe that to fully understand any primary source, one must understand the period of time in which the source was written or recorded. Collected seventy years after the emancipation of American slaves, these narratives had been preserved by the Library of Congress, fortunately, as they were originally created. In 1941, the Library of Congress microfilmed the typewritten pages on which the narratives were originally recorded. In 2001, the Library of Congress digitized the microfilm and made the narratives available on their American Memory web site. From these pages we have reproduced the original documents, including both the marks of the writers of the time and the inconsistencies of the type. Some pages were missing or completely illegible, and we have used a simple typescript provided by the Library of Congress so that the page can be read. Although the font occasionally can make these narratives difficult to read, we believe that it is important not only to preserve the narratives of the slaves but also to preserve the documents themselves, thereby commemorating the groundbreaking effort that produced them. That way, also, we can give you, the reader, not only a collection of the life stories of ex-slaves, but also a glimpse into the time in which these stories were collected, the 1930s.

These are powerful stories by those who lived through slavery. No institution was more divisive in American history than slavery. From the very founding of America and to the present day, slavery has touched us all. We hope these real stories of real lives are preserved for generations of Americans to come.

INFORMANTS

Interview of Mrs. Fannie Berry, Ex-slave
861 E. Bank Street - Petersburg, Virginia
By Susie Byrd, Petersburg, Virginia
Date-----February 26, 1937

NAT TURNER

Back 'fore the sixties, I can 'member my Mistress, Miss Sara Ann, comin' to de window an' hollerin', "De niggers is arisin'! De niggers is arisin'! De niggers is killin' all de white folks, killin' all de babies in de cradle!" It must have been Nat Turner's Insurrection; which wuz sometime 'fo de breakin' of de Civil War.

I wuz waitin' on table in dinin' room an' dis day dey had finished eatin' early an' I wuz cleanin' off table. Don't you know I must have been a good size gal.

JOHN BROWN

Yes, I 'member something 'bout him too. I know my Master came home an' said, dat on his way to de gallows ole John stopped an' kissed a little nigger child. "How com' I don't 'member? Don't tell me I don't 'cause I do. I don't care if its done bin a thousand years ." I know what Master said an' it is as fresh in my mind as it wuz dat day. Dis is de song I herd my Master sing:

> Old John Brown came to Harpers Ferry Town,
> Purpose to raise an insurrection,
> Old Governor Wise put the specks upon his eyes
> An' showed him the happy land of Canaan.

INVENTION

My Master tole us dat de niggers started the railroad, an' dat a

nigger lookin' at a boilin' coffee pot on a stove one day got the idea
dat he could cause it to run by putting wheels on it. Dis nigger being
a blacksmith put his thoughts into action by makin' wheels an' put coffee
on it, an' by some kinder means he made it run an' the idea wuz stole
from him an' dey built de steamengine.

RELATIONSHIP

I wuz one slave dat de poor white man had his match. See Miss Sue?
Dese here ol' white men said, "what I can't do by fair means I'll do by
foul." One tried to throw me, but he couldn't. We tusseled an' knocked
over chairs an' when I got a grip I scratched his face all to pieces; an
dar wuz no more bothering Fannie from him; but oh, honey, some slaves
would be beat up so, when dey resisted, an' sometimes if you'll 'belled
de overseer would kill yo'. Us Colored women had to go through a plenty,
I tell you.

[handwritten left margin: narrative of physical fighting back being effective (compare to solomon norshup)]

[handwritten right margin: trying 'fair' means first?]

MARRIAGE

Elder Williams married me in Miss Delia Mann's (white) parlor on de
crater road. The house still stands. The house wuz full of Colored people.
Miss Sue Jones an' Miss Molley Clark (white), waited on me. Dey took de
lamps an' we walked up to de preacher. One waiter joined my han' an' one
my husband's han'. After marriage de white folks give me a 'ception; an',
honey, talkin' 'bout a table--- hit wuz stretched clean 'cross de dinin'
room. We had everythin' to eat you could call for. No, didn't have no
common eats. We could sing in dar, an' dance ol' squar' dance all us choosed,
ha!ha!ha!Lord! Lord! I can see dem gals now on dat flo'; jes skippin' an' a
trottin'. An' honey, dar wuz no white folks to set down an' eat 'fo you.

WAR

Now, Miss Sue, take up. I jes' like to talk to you, honey 'bout dem days ob slavery; 'cause you look like you wan'ta hear all 'bout 'em. All 'bout de ol' rebels: an' dem niggers who left wid de Yankees an' were sat free, but, poor things, dey had no place to go after dey got freed. Baby, all us wuz helpless an' ain't had nothin'.

I wuz free a long time 'fo' I knew it. My Mistess still hired me out, 'til one day in talkin' to de woman she hired me to, she, "God bless her soul", she told me, "Fannie yo' are free, an' I don't have to pay your Master for you now." You stay with me. She didn't give me no money, but let me stay there an' work for vitals an' clothes 'cause I ain't had no where to go. Jesus, Jesus, God help us! Um, Um, Um ! You Chillun don't know. I didn't say nothin' when she wuz tellin' me, but done 'sided to leave her an' go back to the white folks dat furst own' me.

I plan' to 'tend a big dance. Let me see, I think it wuz on a Thursday night. Some how it tooken got out, you know how gals will talk an' it got to ol' Bil Duffeys ears (ol' dog an', baby do you know, mind you 'twont slavery time, but de 'oman got so mad cause I runned away from her dat she get a whole passel of 'em out looking for me. Dar wuz a boy, who heard 'em talkin' an' sayin' dey wuz goin' to kill me if I were found. I will never forget dis boy com' up to me while I wuz dancin' wid another man an' sed, "nobody knowes where you ar', Miss Moore, dey is lookin' fer you, an' is gwine kill you, so yo' come on wid me." Have mercy, have mercy my Lord, honey, you kin jes 'magin' my feelin' fer a minute. I couldn't move. You know de gals an' boys all got 'round me an' told me to go wid Squreball, dat he would show me de way to my old Mistess house. Out we took, an' we ran one straight mile up de road, den through de woods, den we had to go through a straw field. Dat field seem' like three miles.

4

After den, we met another skit of woods. Miss Sue, baby my eyes, (ha!ha!ha!)
wuz bucked an' too if it is setch a thin' as being so scared yo' hair stand
on yo' head, I know, mine did. An' dat wasn't all, dat boy an' me puffed
an' sweated like bulls. Was feared to stop, cause we might have been
tracked.

At last we neared de house an' I started throwin' rocks on de porch.
Child I look an' heard dat white 'oman when she hit dat floor, bouncin' out
dat bed she mus' felt dat I wuz comin' back to her. She called all de men
an' had 'em throw a rope to me an' day drawed me up a piece to le window,
den I held my arms up an' dey snatched me in.   Honey, Squreball fled to
de woods. I ain't never heard nothin' 'bout him. An' do you know, I didn't
leave day 'oman's house no more for fifteen years?

Lord! Lord!honey, Squreball an' I use to sing dis song.

"Twas 1861, the Yankees made de Rebels run

We'll all go stone blin'

When de Johny's come a marchin' home.

Child an' here's another one we use to sing. 'Member de war donk
bin when we would sing dese songs. Listen now:

Ain't no more blowin' of dat four
day horn

I will sing, brethern, I will sing.

A col' frosty mornin' de nigger's
mighty good

Take your ax upon your shoulder.

Nigger talk to de woods,

Ain't no mor' blowin' of dat four
day horn.

I will sing brethern, I will sing.

SONG

Kimo, Kimo, dar you are

Heh, hoy rump to pume did'dle.

Set back pinkey wink,

Come Tom Nippecat

Sing song Kitty cat, can't

You carry me o'er?

$$\overline{2}$$

Up de darkies head so bold

Sing song, Kitty, can't you

Carry me O'er?

Sing Song, Kitty, can't yo'

Carry me home?

I wuz at Pamplin an' de Yankees an' Rebels were fightin' an' dey were wavin' the bloody flag an' a confederate soldier wuz upon a post an' they were shootin' terribly. Guns were firin' everywhere.

All a sudden dey struck up Yankee Doodle Song. A soldier came along and called to me, " How far is it to the Rebels", an I honey, wuz feared to tell him, So, I said, "I don't know", He called me again. Scared to death, I recollect gittin' behind the house an' pointed in the direction. You see, ef de Rebels knew dat I told the soldier, they would have killed me.

These were the Union men goin' after Lee's army which had don' bin 'fore dem to Appomattox.

The Colored regiment came up behind an' when they saw the Colored regiment they put up the white flag. (Yo' 'member 'fo' dis red or bloody flag was up). Now, do you know why dey raised dat white flag? Well, honey, dat white flag wuz a token dat Lee, had surrendered.

Glory! Glory! yes, child the Negroes are free, an' when they knew dat dey were free dey, Oh! Baby! began to sing:

> Mamy don't yo' cook no mo',
> Yo' ar' free, yo' ar' free.
> Rooster don't yo' crow no, mo'
> Yo' ar' free, yo' ar' free,
> Ol' hen, don't yo' lay no mo' eggs
> Yo' free, yo' free.

Sech rejoicing an' shoutin', you never he'rd in you' life.

Yes, I can recollect de blowin' up of the Crater. We had fled, but I do know 'bout the shellin' of Petersburg. We left Petersburg when de shellin' commenced an' went to Pamplin in box cars, gettin' out of de way. Dem were scared times too, cause you looked to be kilt any minute by stray bullets. Just before the shellin' of Petersburg, dey were sellin' niggers for little nothin' hardly.

Junius Broadie, a white man bought some niggers, but dey didn't stay slave long, cause de Yankees came an' set 'em free.

450003

THE STORY OF CHARLES CRAWLEY, EX-SLAVE

God knows, how old I am. All I know is, I wuz born 'fore de war.

Yes, I wuz a slave an' belonged to a family of Allen's in Luenburg County, came here to dis Petersburg de second week of Lee's surrender.

My Marster and Mistess wuz good to me as well as all us slaves. Dey owned 'bout fifty head of Colored People. All de work I did wuz to play an' drive cows, being only a boy worked around as chillun; doin' dis, an' dat, little things de white folks would call me to do.

Marster Allen, owned my Mother, an' sister too; we emigrant (emigrated) here, came to dis town of Petersburg after Lee's surrender, I mean you know de ending of de Civil War. My mother, sister, and I came on down de road in a box car, which stopped outside de outskirts; hit didn't go through de city. Yes, I know when de first railroads were built, de Norfolk and Western an' de Atlantic Coast Line, dey were run through Petersburg an' in dem days it wuz called de Southern.

Mis and Mars' Allen didn't want us to leave dat part of de Country to come to dis here place down de road, but we comed ourselves to make a home fo' ourselves. Well now, we worked here an' dar, wid dis here man an' dat man; o, well, wid different people 'til we bought us selves a home an' paid for it. Mother died right here in dis here house; twelve years ago, dis comin' March 'leventh. I am yet livin' in dis same house, dat she an' us all labored an'

worked fo' by de sweat of our brow, an' wid dese hands, Lord! Lord!

Child dem days wuz some days. Let me finish baby, tellin' you 'bout

dis house. De groun' wuz bought from a lady (Colored) name Sis

Jackey, an' she wuz sometimes called in dem days de Mother of Har-

rison Street Baptis' Church. I reckon dis church is de ol'est one

in Petersburg.

O, yes, honey, I can 'member when de Yankees came into dis town;

day broke in stores an' told all de niggers to go in an' git enything

dey wanted.

When slaves ran away they were brought back to their Master and

Mistess; when dey couldn't catch 'em they didn't bother, but let 'em

go. Sometimes de slaves would go an' take up an' live at tother

places; some of 'em lived in de woods off of takin' things, sech as

hogs, corn, an' vegetables from other fo'ks farm. Well, if dese slaves

wuz cought, dey were sold by their New Masters to go down south. Dey

tell me dem Masters down South, wuz so mean to slaves dey would let

'em work dem cotton fields 'til dey fall dead wid hoes in dare hands,

'en would beat dem. I'm glad to say, we had good owners.

There wus a auction block, I saw right here in Petersburg on the

corner of Sycamore street and Bank street. Slaves were auctioned off

to de highest bidder. Some refused to be sold, by dat I mean, "cried".

Lord! Lord! I done seen dem young'uns fout and kick like crazy fo'ks;

Child it wuz pitiful to see 'em. Den dey would handcuff an' beat 'em

unmerciful. I don' like to talk 'bout back dar. It brun' a sad feelin'

up me. If slaves 'belled, I done seed dem whip 'em wid a strop cal'

"cat mine tails." Honey, dis strop wuz 'bout broad as yo' hand, from

thum' to little finger, an' 'twas cut in strips up. Yo' done seen dese
whips dat they whip horses wid? Well dey was used too.

You sed somethin' 'bout how we served God. Um, um, child, I tell
you jest how we use to do. We use to worship at different houses. You
see you would git a remit to go to dese places. You would have to show
your remit. If de Pattyrollers, caught you dey would whip yo'. Dats
de wa' dey done in dem da's. Pattyrollers, is a gang of white men gitting together goin' through de country catching slaves, an' whipping an'
beatin' 'em up if dey had no remit. Marster Allen wouldn't 'llow no
one to whip an' beat his slaves, an' he would handle anybody if dey did;
so, Marster's slaves met an' worshipped from house to house, an honey,
we talked to My God all us wanted.

You know we use to call Marster Allen, Colonel Allen. His name wuz
Robert. He wuz a home general, an' a lawyer, too. When he went to court
any slave he said to free, wuz freed an' turned aloose. De white fo'ks
as well as slaves obeyed Marster Allen.

Did you know poor whites like slaves had to git a pass? I mean, a
remit like as slaves, to sell anythin' an' to go places, or do anythin'.
Jest as we Colored people, dey had to go to some big white man like
Colonel Allen, dey did . If Marster wanted to, he would give dem a remit
or pass, an' if he didn't feel like it, he wouldn't do it. It wuz jes as
he felt 'bout hit. Dats what made all feared him. Ol' Marster wuz
more hard on dem poor white fo'ks den he wuz on us niggers. contemporary comparison

I don't know but two sets of white fo'ks slaves up my way; one was
name Chatman, an' de tother one Nellovies. Dese two families worked on
Allen's farm as we did. Off from us on a plot called Morgan's lot,
there dey lived as slaves jes like us Colored fo'ks. Yes de poor white
man had some dark an' tough days, like us poor niggers; I mean werl

perception &
abolition wasn't
necessarily
permanent?

lashed an' treated, some of 'em, jes as pitiful an' unmerciful. Lord!
Lord! baby, I hope yo' young fo'ks will never know what slavery is, an'
will never suffer as yo' foreparents. O God! God! I'm livin' to tell
de tale to yo', honey. Yes, Jesus, yo've spared me.

For clothin' we were 'llowed two suits a year - one fer spring, an'
one fer winter, was all yo' had. De underclothes were made at home.
Yo' also got two pairs of shoes an' homemade hats an' caps. The white
fo'ks or your slave owners would teach dem who could catch on easy an'
dey would teach de other slaves, an' dats how dey kept all slaves
clothed. Our summer hats were made out of plaited straw. Underclothes
made out of sacks an' bags.

We had plenty of food sech as 'twas, cornbread, butter milk, sweet
potatoes in week days. Ha! Ha! honey, guess dats why niggers don't
like cornbread today; dey got a dislike for dat bread from back fo'ks.
On Sunday we had biscuits, and sometimes a little extra food, which ol'
Mistess would send out to Mother fer us.

Fer as I think, if slavery had lasted, it would have been pretty
tough. As it was, some fared good, while others fared common. You know,
slaves who were beat an' treated bad; some of dem had started gittin' together an' killin' de white folks when dey carried dem out to de field to
work. God is punishin' some of dem ol' suckers an' their chillun right
now fer de way dey use to treat us poor Colored fo'ks.

I think by Negro gittin' educated he has profited, an' dis here
younger generation is gwine to take nothin' off dese here poor white fo'ks
when dey don't treat dem right, cause now dis country is a free country; no
slavery now.

Interview of Mrs. Minnie Fulkes - 459 E Byrne Street
Petersburg, Virginia
By -- Susue Byrd
March 5, 1937

I was born the twenty fifth of December and I am 77 years old. My mother was a slave and she belonged to Dick Belcher in Chesterfield County. Old Dick sold us again to Gelaspe Graves. 'member now fifteen of mother's chillun went with her having de same master. *emotive language repeating*

Honey, I don't like to talk 'bout dem times, 'cause my mother did suffer misert. You know dar wus an' overseer who use to tie mother up in de barn with a rope aroun' her arms up over her head, while she stood on a block. Soon as dey got her tied, dis block was moved an' her feet dangled, yo' know, couldn't tech de flo'.

Dis ol' man, now, would start beatin' her nekkid 'til the blood run down her back to her heels. I took an' seed th' whelps an' scars fer my own self wid dese here two eyes. (this whip she said, "was a whip like dey use to use on horses; it wuz a peice of leather 'bout as wide as my han' from little finger to thumb). After dey had beat my muma all dey wanted another overseer. Lord, Lord, I hate white people and de flood waters gwine drown some mo. Well honey dis man would bathe her in salt and water. Don't you kno' dem places wuz a hurtin'. Um, um. *sadism*

V. different from previous account

I asked mother , what she done fer 'en to beat and do her so? She said, "nothin', tother than she refused to be wife to dis man."

An' muma say, "If he didn't treat her dis way a dozen times, it wasn't nary one."

immediate power of overseer

Mind you, now muma's marster didn't know dis wuz going on. You know, if slaves would tell, why dem overseers would kill 'em.

An' she sed dat dey use to have meetings an' sing and pray an' th' ol' paddy rollers would hear dem, so to keep th' sound from goin' out, slaves would

abstracting owner from violence → easier to see benevolent figure

-2-

great

put a gra' big iron pot at the door, an' you know some times dey would fer git

to put ol' pot dar an' the paddy rollers would come an' horse whip every las' one

of 'em, jes cause poor souls were praying to God to free 'em from dat awful bondage.

Ha! ha! ha! dar wuz one ol' brudder who studied fer 'em one day an' tol

all de slaves how to git even wid 'em.

more
violence
!

He tol' 'em to tie grape vines an' other vines across th' road, den when de

Paddy rollers come galantin' wid their horses runnin' so fast you see dem vines

would tangle 'em up an' cause th' horses to stumble and fall. An' lots of times,

badly dey would break dere legs and horses too; one interval one ol' poor devil

got tangled so an' de horse kept a carryin' him, 'til he fell off horse and next

day a sucker was found in road whar dem vines wuz wind aroun' his neck so many

times yes had chok ed him, dey said, "he totely dead. Serve him right 'cause dem

ol' white folks treated us so mean.

Well, some times, you know dey would, the others of 'em, keep going 'til

dey fin' whar dis meeting wuz gwine on. Dey would come in and start whippin' an'

beatin' the slaves unmerciful. All dis wuz done to keep yo' from servin' God, an'

do you know some of dem devils wuz mean an' sinful 'nough to say. "Ef I ketch you

here agin servin' God I'll beat you. You haven't time to serve God. We bought you

to serve us. Um, um.

God's gwine 'rod dem wicket marsters. Ef hit 'taint 'em whut gits hit,

hits gonna fall on deir chillun.

In dem back days child, meetings wuz carried on jes like we do today, some -

whatly. Only difference is the slave dat knowed th' most 'bout de Bible would tell

and explain what God had told him in a vision (yo' young folks say, "dream")

dat dis freedom would come to pass; an' den dey prayed fer dis vision to come to

pass, an' dars whar de paddy rollers would whip 'em ag'in.

Lord! Lord dey, pew! pew! pew! Baby, "I jes kno' I could if I knowed how

to write, an' had a little learning I could put off a book on dis here situation.
Yo' kno what I mean 'bout dese way back questions yo' is a asking me to tell yo'
'bout; as fer as I can recollect in my mind.

When Graves bought us, he sold three of us an' three slaves. My brother an'
sister went down south. Muma sed to de cotton country an' too, she say, "they were
made to wrok in th' cotton fields by their new marster, out in dem white fields in
th' brawlin' sun from th' time it breaked day 'till yo' couldn't see at night an',
yes indeedy,an' if God isn't my right'ous judge they were given not half to eat,
no not 'nough, to eat. Dey wuz beaten ef dey ask'd for any mo'".

As to marriage, when a slave wanted to marry, why he would jes ask his marster
to go over and ask de tother marster could he take un te himself dis certain gal
fer a wife. Mind you now, all de slaves dat marster called out of quarters an' he'd
make 'em line up see, stand in a row like soldiers, and de slave man is wid his
marster when dis askin' is gwine on, and he pulls de gal to him he wants;an' de
marster den make both jump over broom stick an' after dey does, dey is pronounced
man an' wife, both stayin' wid same marsters (I mean ef John Marris Sallie~John
stay wid his ol' marster an' Sal' wid hers,but had privileges, you know,like
married folks; an' ef chillun were born all of 'em, no matter how many, belonged
to de marster whar de woman stayed.

If I aint made a mistake, I think it wuz in April when de war surrendered
an' muma an' all us wuz turned aloose in May. Yes dat ol' wench, a ol' heifer,
oh child, it makes my blood bile when I think 'bout it. Yes she kept muma igrunt.
Didn't tell her nuthing 'bout being free 'til den in May.

Den her mistess, Miss Betsy Godsey, tol' her she wuz free, an' she (muma)
coul' cook fer her jes th' same dat she would give her something to eat an' help
clothe us chillun, dat wuz ef muma continual' to sta wid her an' work.

You see, we didn't have nuthin' an' no whar to go, um,um,um so we all, you
know, jes took en stayed 'til we wuz able wid God's help to pull us selves te—
gether. But my God it wuz 'ginst our will, but, baby, couldn't help ourselves.

My fathers master tol' him he could farm one haf fer th' tother an'
when time rolled 'roun' fer dem 'viding crops he took an' give to him his part
like any honest man would do. Ah, Lord child, dem wuz terrible times too, oh!
it makes me shudder when I think of some slaves had to stay in de woods an' git
long best way dey could after freedom done bin' clared; you see slaves who had
mean master would rather be dar den whar dey lived. By an' by God opened a way
an' dey got wid other slaves who had huts. You see, after th' render no white
folks could keep slaves. Do yo' know even now, honey, an' dat done bin way bac'
yonder, dese ol' white folks think us poor colored people is made to work an'
slave fer dem, look! dey aint give you no wages worth nuthin'. Gal cook all week
fer two an' three dollars. How can you live off it, how kin, yer kin yo'?

My father waited on soldiers and after de s'render dey carried him an'
his brother as fer as Washington D.C. I think we all use to say den,"Washington
City. Aint you done heard folks talk 'bout dat city? 'Tis a grade big city,
daus whar de President of dis here country stay; an' in bac' days it wuz known
as 'vidin' lin' fer de North an' South. I done hear dem white folks tell all
'bout dem things, dis line. As I wuz tellin' you, hos brother wuz kept, but dey
sent father bac' home. Uncle Spencer wuz left in Prince Williams County. All
his chillun ar' still dar. I don't know de name of Yankee who carried him off.

Lord, Lord, Honey, dem times too over sad 'cause Yankees took lots of
slaves away an' dey made homes, An' whole heap of families lost sight of each
other. I know of a case whar after hit wuz ten years a brother an' sister
lived side by side an' didn't know dey wuz blood kin.

My views 'bout de chillun in dem bac' days is dat dese here chillun
what is now comin' up is too pisen brazen fer me.

Now jes' lem me tell you how I did I marred when I wuz 14 years old.
So help me God, I didn't know what marriage meant. I had an idea when you loved
de man, you an' he could be married an' his wife had to cook, clean up, wash,
an' iron fer him was all. I slept in bed he on his side an' I en mine fer

three months an' dis aint no lie. Miss Sue, he never got close to me 'cause
muma had sed "Don't let no body bother yo' principle, 'cause dat wuz all yo'
had. I 'bey my muma, an' tol' him so, and I said to go an' ask muma an' ef she
sed he could get close to me hit was alright. An" he an' I went to gether to see
and ask muma.

Den muma said "Come here chillun, and she began tellin' me to please my husband,
an' 'twas my duty as a wife, dat he had marred a pu'fect lady."

importance of bodily integrity: reputation

Dese here chillun don't think of deir principle. Run purfectly wild. Old
women too. Dey ain't all 'em true to one, but have two.

Jes what is gittin' in to dis generation; is hit de worl ' comin' to an end?

Ha! had ha! I goin ' tel' yo' som'thin' else.

I had a young man to come to see me one evenin' an' he sed dis to me,
"Miss Moore" "Let me jin my fence to your plantation."

I give him his hat. I say, "no" yo' go yo' way an' I go mine. I wuz through
wid him, an' mind yo' I from dat da' 'til dis aint knowed what he wuz talkin'
'bout an' wuz ashamed to ask muma; but I thought he insulted me."

I didn't never go to school. Had to work an' am working now an' when hit
breaks good weather, I go fishing. And who works dat big garden out dar? No body
but me."

You know I'm mother of eleven chillun, an' 'tis seven living an' four of
dem ded.

Interview of Mrs. Georgina Giwbs, Ex-slave
By -- Thelma Dunston
Portsmouth, Virginia
January 15, 1937

APR 14 1937

        Mrs. Georgina Giwbs, an ex-slave, resides at 707 Lindsey Avenue, Portsmouth,

Virginia. The old lady marveled at the great change that has been made in the

clothings, habits and living conditions of the Negro since she was a child. She

described the clothing of the slaves in a calm manner, "All of de cloth during

slavery time was made on de loom. My mastah had three slaves who worked in de

loom house. After de cloth was made, mastah sent hit over town to a white woman

who made hit in clothes. We had to knit all our stockings and gloves. We'd plait

blades of wheat to make us bonnets. We had to wear wooden bottom shoes. Dere won't

no stores, so we growed everything we et, an' we'd make everything we'd wear."

        "We had a washing house. Dere wuz five women who done de washing an' ironing.

Dey had to make de soap. Dat wuz done by letting water drip over oak ashes. Dis

made oak ash lye, and dis wuz used in making soap. After de clothes had soaked

in dis lye-soap and water, dey put de clothes on tables and beat 'em 'till dey

wuz white."

        "Mastah give us huts to live in. De beds wuz made of long boards dat wuz

nailed to de wall. De mattress wuz stuffed wif straw and pine tags. De only light

we had wuz from de fire-place. We didn't use no matches, 'stead we'd strick a

rock on a piece of steel. We'd let the sparks fall on some cotton."

        "My mastah had 'bout five hundred slaves. He'd never sell none of his slaves,

but he'd always buy more. Dat keeps de slaves from marrying in dere famblies. When   *a breeding practice*

yer married, yer had to jump over a broom three times. Dat wuz de licence. Ef mastah

seen two slaves together too much he would marry them. Hit didn't make no difference

ef yer won't but fourteen years old." *enforced marriage and another behavior to control*

        "Work began at sun rise and last 'till sun down. When I wuz eight years old,

I started working in de field wif two paddles to keep de crows from eatin' de crops.

theme of constant observation permeating

We had a half day off on Sunday, but you won't 'lowed to visit. Sometimes de men slaves would put logs in de beds, and dey'd cover 'em up, den dey go out. Mastah would see de logs and think dey wuz de slaves."

"My father told me dere wuz once a mastah who sold a slave woman and her son. Many years after dis, de woman married. One day when she wuz washing her husband's back she seen a scar on his back. De woman 'membered de scar. It wuz de scar her mastah had put on her son. 'Course dey didn't stay married, but de woman wouldn't ever let her son leave her."

Superstitions told by Mrs. Georgina Giwbs   love

1. "Ef a dog turns on his back and howls', 'tis a sign of death."

2. "Ef yer drops a dish rag on de floor and it spreads out, 'tis de sign dat a hungry woman is gwine ter come to yer house. Ef de rag don't spread out den a hungry man is a coming."

3. "Ef a black cat crosses yer path going to de right, 'tis good luck. Ef de cat goes to de left 'tis bad luck."

4. Ef a girl walks aroung wif one shoe off and one on, she'll stay single as many years as de number of steps she taken.

450006

Interview of Mrs. Candis Goodwin
Aged 80
Cape Charles, Virginia

systematic devaluation of self worth

denial of personal histories

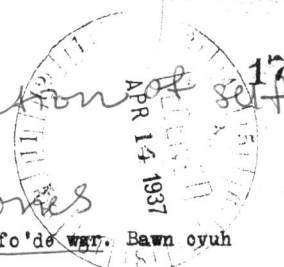

Ah ain't knowd, 'xactly, how ol' ah is, but ah bawn 'fo'de war. Bawn oyuh

yonder at Seaview, on ol' Masser Scott's plantation. Tain't fur f'om here. Yes,

reckon ah 'bout six yeah ol' when de Yankees come, jes' a lil' thin', you know.

language of ownership My white people dey good tuh me. Cose dey gits mad wid you but dey don' beat

non o' us; jes' ack lak it. Why, ah was jes lak dey's chullun; ah played wid 'em,

et wid 'em an' eb'n slep' wid 'em. Ah kinder chillish, ah reckon. Had muh own way.

Muh mommer, she wuck in de quater kitchen. She ain' ha'tuh wuck hawd lak some. Had

it kinder easy, too. Jes' lak ah tells yuh ah al'ys had my way. Ah gits whut ah

wants an' ef'n dey don't gi' tuh me, ah jes' teks it.

No neber had no wuck to do in dem days 'ceptin' nursin' de babies. 'Twas

jes' lak play; twan no wuck. Uster go ober to Nottingham's tuh play, go long wid

Missus chillun, yuh know. Ah laks tuh go ober there cause dey has good jam an'

biscuits. Ef'n dey don gi' me none, ah jes' teks some. Dey don do nuttin'; jes'

say, "Tek yuh han' out dat plate". But ah got whut ah wants den. Why we chillun

user hab a time 'round ol' Missus' place. All us chillun uster git togeder an'

go in de woods tuh play. Yes, de white and black uns, too. De grea' big whi' boys

uster go 'long wid us, too. Know how we play? We tek de brown pine shadows an'

mek houses outer 'em an' den mek grass outer de green uns. Den we go ober Missus'

dairy and steal inything we want an' tek it to our houses in de woods. Dem was

good ol' times, ah tel yuh, honey.

play / fun w/ enslavers

Tel yuh, whut ah uster do. Ah uster play pranks on ol' Massed Scott. Ah's

regular lil' devil, ah was. Come night, ev'y body sit 'round big fire place in

living room. Soon it git kinder late, Massa git up outer his cheer tuh win' up

de clock. Ah gits hin' his cheer ret easy, an' quick sneak his cheer f'om un'er

him; an' when he finish he set smack on de flow! Den he say "Dogone yuh lil'

cattin', ah gwan switch yuh!" Ah jes' fly out de room. Won't sceared though cause ah knows Massa won' gon do nottin' 'tuh me.

What ah know 'bout whippin' . Well ah ain' had uh whippin' in my life. But ah hear tel o' how dey whips um though. Yuh know dey uster tek dat cowhide an' cut 'em till dey backs beeds. Some jes' lak see de blood run down. Better not cry neider. Mek yuh holler, "Oh pray! oh pray!" Couldn't say nottin' else. But Massa Scott neber had none dat kinder stuff on his place. He say tain't right. Didn't 'low no paddyrollers 'round eider. Say dey "trechous". Massa Nottin'ham neber had 'em on his place neider. He didn' neber strike one o' his niggers; nobody else better not neider.

Honey, ah teh yuh ah growd jes' as good's Any chil' in dis country. Ol' Missus Scott gimme good clothes; cose ah didn't git 'em mone twice a yeah, but dey's good when ah gits 'em. She gimmie Sis' dresses. Sis' one ob Missus' lil'le girls. An' de whi' chillun dey learn me how tuh read, too. Cose de whi' folks din wan' yuh to learn. Ah 'member jes' as clare as yestidy how one dem chillun learn me how tuh read "compress-i-bility". Thought ah was suppin' den! Ah kin read Bible lil'a now but ah can' write; neber learn tuh write.

Did ah eber go tuh church? Cose ah did! Went ret 'long wid Missus' chillun. Had tuh set in de back, but dat won' nottin'. My mommer, she went tuh church too. Sometime de ol' folk uster git togeder in de quater-kitchen tuh shout an' pray. Dats where my mommer git 'ligion. She kinder tender 'oman couldn' stan' dat preachin' no longer.

What 'bout muh pappy? Dat's suppin' ah ain' tol' yuh 'bout. Well, yuh know uncle Stephen, he kinder overseer fo' some widow 'omans. He Mommer husband. He come see muh mommer Any time he gits ready. But ah fin' out he ain' muh pappy. Ah knowd dat since when ah's a lil' thin'. Ah uster go ovur tuh massa William's plantation. Dey tell me all 'bout. De folks ober dere dey uster say tuh me, "Who's yuh pappy? Who's yuh pappy?" Ah jes' say "Tuckey buzzard lay me an' de sun hatch me" an' den gwan 'bout my business. Cose all de time dey knows an' ah knows

too dat Massa Williams was muh pappy. Ah tell yuh suppin' else. Got uh brother
libin' ret on dis here street; one dem toof doctors, yuh know what pulls yer teef.
Cose he's white. But tain't knowed 'roun' here. 'Twould ruin him. He's a nice man
though. Uster go tuh see muh son an' his wife, lots uh times. Yes dey's good frien!ss

Yes, dey had overseers. Sometime dey call dem stewards. Had colored uns too.
Massa Scott had white overseers, good man though; but Massa Nottin'ham, he had big
black boss on his place. cain' 'member his name. He ain' had to git no p'mission
tuh come tuh our place. He jes' come an' goes when he gits ready.

Kin ah 'member de war? Yes, indeed! 'Member jes' lak 'twas yestidy. Well
dey had a stow down de conner f'om Massa's plantation, an' de al'ys sen' me tuh
stow fo' tuh buy things. Uster go down dere an' dem Yankees be sittin' all 'long
de road wid dey blue coats, ret pretty site; twas. But ah's sceard tuh deaf, when
ah gits neah 'em. Ah gits what ah wants f'om de stow, an' flys pass 'em. Dem Yankees
show had dey way. Dey went in all de white folks house; tek dey silver, an' inything
dey big 'nough carry out. Jes' ruin Missus furniture; get up on de table an' jes'
cut capper. Nasty things! Den de Yankees goes 'round at night tek anybody dey wants
tuh help 'em fight. Twas dey "Civil right". Got my Jake, cose ah neber knowd him
den. He twelve yeah oller ah is.

Lemmie tell yuh 'bout muh Jake, how he did in de war. He big man in dey war.
He drill soldiers ev'y day. Firs' he be in one dem companies - Company "C" ah
bliebe. Den he wucked up to be sergent-Major, in de Tenth Regiment. Jacob ~~Godium~~
his name was. He say all look up tuh him an' 'spect him too. See dat "Sowd" ov'in
dat coner, dat's de ve'y sowd he used in de war, an' ah kep' it all dese yeahs.
No de soldiers neber did no fighting 'round here's ah know of. But plenty ob 'em
camped here.

My Jake, he hansome man, he was. 'Member, how we firs' got togeder. We all   *early*
was tuh church one Sunday, an' Jake he kep' cidin' up to me. An' ah lookin' at him   *relationships*
outer de coner muh eye, till finally he come up an' took holt muh han's. 'Twas af't
de war ah had growd up. Ah was in muh early teens den. Dey say ah's de purtiet girl
on de Shore. An' when Jake an' me got married, ev'ybody said, "You show meks a purty

couple."

De ol' Scott chillun what ah growd up wid? No, mone dem lef' now. Dey las'
girl died heah las' yeah an' hur daughter come way down here f'om up in Maryland
tuh tell "An' Candis" 'bout it. Wouldn' tell me sceard 'twould 'cite me. But ah hea'd
hur tellin' my chil dere all 'bout it. Ol' Massa Scott's chillun, some dem, dey still
comes tuh see me. Slip me some money now'n den, an' suppin' t'eat, too. Dey's all
moughty nice folks, dem Scotts is.

Interview of Mr. Charles Grandy, Ex-slave
David Hoggard
February 26, 1937

Norfolk, Va. —

APR 14 1937

450011

History of Ex-slave and Civil War Veteran

Charles Grandy was born February 19, 1842, in Mississippi. While still an infant, he was brought to Norfolk. When the family arrived in Norfolk his father was arrested on some pretentious charge, and the whole family was placed in prison. After their release , they were taken to a plantation near Hickory Ground, Virginia, and sold. Slaves, at this time, were often taken to rural districts in carts, and sold to owners of plantations, as they were needed. Family life, friendships, and love affairs were often broken up; many times never to be united.

Following the general routine of slaves, the Grandy family was given a shanty; food and clothing was also issued to them, and had to last until the master decided to give out another supply. Usually, he issued them their allowance of food weekly. Often the supply was insufficient for their needs.

Charles played around the plantation "big house", doing small errands until he reached the age of five, then his play days ended. While playing on the wood pile one morning, his master called him, "boy do you see this grass growing along the side of the fence? Well pull it al up." When his first task was finished, he was carried to the field to pull the grass from the young cotton and other growing crops. This work was done by hand because he was still too young to use the farm implements. Now he want to his task daily; from early in the morning until late in the evening. The long toilsome days completely exhausted the youngster. Often he would fall asleep before reaching home, and spend a good portion of the night on the bare ground. Awakening, he would find it quite a problem to locate his home in the darkness of night.

age

rite of passage?

Such good illustration of childhood

From the stage of grass pulling by hand, he grew strong enough, in a few years, to use the hoe rake and sickle. While attempting to carry out his masters orders to cut corn tassels with a large sharp knife, his elbow was seriously cut. He was taken to the house and treated, the application being chimmey soot, to stop the bleeding. After this treatment the arm was placed in a sling, and eventually became deformed from insufficient care. He was sent back to the fields to pick cotton, with one free hand and his teeth, while painfully carrying the other hand in the sling. Failing to obey this command, he would have been given a whipping, or sent to the southlands. Sending slaves to the plantations of Mississippi and other southern states was a type of punishment all slaves feared.

Slaves were not allowed much freedom of worship. The Yankee soldiers and officers played a great part in the slave's moral training, and religious worship. They secretly instructed small gatherings of slaves, at night. The points stressed most were, obedience and the evils of stealing. There were some sections where masters were liberal in their views toward their slaves, and permitted them to worship openly.

Slaves were allowed to have small quantities of whiskey, even during the days of their worship, to use for medicinal purposes. It was a common occurrence to see whiskey being sold at the foot of the hill near the churchyard.

The news of war, and the possibility of Negroes enlisting as soldiers was truly a step closer to the answering of their prayers for freedom. Upon hearing of this good news Grandy joined a few of the others in this break for freedom. One night, he and a close friend packed a small quantity of food in a cloth and set out about midnight to join the northern army. Traveling at night most of the time, they were constantly confronted with the danger of being recaptured. Successfully eluding their followers, they reached Portsmouth after many narrow escapes. From Portsmouth they moved to Norfolk.

Arriving in Norfolk, Grandy and his friend decided to take different roads of travel. Several days and nights found him wandering about the outskirts of Norfolk, feeding on wild berries, etc. While picking berries along a ditch bank, he was hailed by a Yankee soldier, who having come in contact with run away slaves before, greeted him friendly, and questioned him of his home and of his knowledge of work. He was taken to camp and assigned as cook. At first, he was not very successful in his job, but gradually improvement was shown. He was asked what wages he would accept. It was such a pleasure to know that he had escaped the clutches of slavery, he did not ask for wages; but instead, he was willing to work for anything they would give him, no matter how small, as long as he didn't have to return to slavery.

Within a short period he was given a uniform and gun; was fully enlisted as a soldier, in the 19th regiment of Wisconsin, Company E. Here he remained in service until November, 1862, after which time he returned to Norfolk to spend some time with his mother, who was still living. While sitting in the doorway one day, with his Mother, he was again confronted with the proposition of reenlisting. He agreed to do so for one year, to serve as guard at Fortress Monroe. He remained there until the close of the War, offering brave and faithful services.

Mr. Grandy is now ninty-five years old, residing at 609 Smith Street, Norfolk, Virginia. He is still able to attend the various conventions of Civil War Veterans. He can read, write, and has a fair knowledge of the Bible. His main interest is the organization of Negroes into strong groups. He enjoys talking about religion and is quite an interesting and intelligent person to talk with.

450005

Interview of Mrs. Della Harris
2 - E Byrne Street
Petersburg, Virginia
By -- Susie Byrd
February 5, 1937

B-2 ; **24**

v. collaborative process

I don't know just how old I is. Muma sent me to private school wid white
chillun fo' one week. I was 13 years old at de time uh Lee's surrender. I belong
to Peter or Billy Buck Turnbull Warrenton, N.C. Put this down. My mother and family
all belong to Peter Buck as his slaves. We didn't work until after the war; then we
came to Petersburg. I went to dancing school wid the white folks and can dance any
kind of dance sets. My father was a musicianer. He belonged to John Carthan, in
Warrenton, N.C. In dem days you had to take your Master's and Mistess' name. In slavery
time when a slave married he had to ask his Moster and Mistess.

"We never went to church. We used to hear de bells ringing loud, baby, yes,
clear and strong. No, never seen no Sunday school, and the first time I went in a church
I looked all around, and baby, I thought dat I was in heaven. It wasn't long, Miss
Sue, before I got 'legeon, and, yes, I jined de church, 15 years old I wuz. Never will
forget the time, or dat place. Den I lived here with an ant, muma's sister, who was
named Kate Williams. Her husband wuz my uncle, and he worked and died at de White
House in Washington City.

" I don't know de name of de President he worked for, but you can find dat
out on dem books. You know you young folks calls um records.

"Yes child I'm proud of my age never gave no body no trouble.

I have 8 children dead and now only one son living. Peter Turnbull was good
to all his slaves, as far as I know. Mama was a cook in slavery time. She died in
Petersburg, yes, right here in dis hole.

"No muma never owned any thing, always rented and aint never owned nothing but
a passel of children.

"My muma was a geniune Indian. Some people say you can't own Indians. I don't
know how cum, but I do know she was owned by these people, but she surely was an
Indian. Every body knows me all over Virginia.

"When I use to be in dinning room service I would hear de white folks talk, and, do you know, Miss Sue you can hear a lot that way?

"Moster said he couldn't sell me 'cause I was so little, just kept me fur to wait on de little chillun in de house.

"Miss Sue, you'll have to give me something for telling you all dis here, if it ain't nothing but a horse cake.

"I've seen lots of dis world in travel. Done bin to Baltimore City; done bin to Philadelphia.

"I aint gwine give you no more, gal.

"Yes, to Lynchburg, den I worked at Mont Royal School, Baby , where Mrs McDaniel was manager.

"The man gwine say, "dat woman bin some where." If I stayed long enough I might a got some learning but I stayed only one year. Got tired of that place. From one season to another is a year, aint it? Ah ! Lord!

"Young folks now adays are just fur a good time, and a good time too they have. Yes, Siree Bob!

"Gwine stop now, Miss Sue, aint gwine give you no mo'. Man gwine say, Miss Sue, where in the devil did you get this stuff? Gal, you are a mess. You gonna write most all dat book about Della. Go on now, dats nough.

"In dem days chillun were chillun, now every body is grown. Chillun then were seen and not heard. When old persons came around muma sent us out and you better not be seen. Now every body act grown. Make the man laugh.

"I've always enjoyed good health. Never had a Doctor in my life, not even when my chillun wuz born. Dis rubbing when people got pain just rubs it in. Eating so much and late hours is cause you young folks dying. All muma's chillun wuz healthy. "Real Food in dem days, yes, muma fed us good vituals from white folks. I tell you, we had good owners. I didn't see sun set when I wuz a child. Always went to bed early,

illustrative, contrast with previous account

child, I wish I could call back dem days, Muma said people lived so much longer because they took care of themselves.

"All dis here education an' people just now got it."

Question: Do you think, Mrs. Harris, education has helped our race?

"Well, child, I don' know, Folks are so indifferent now I am afraid to say. Pshaw.. Colored folks now, some are messy, don't know how to be polite.

"Talking about lightning days, Its lightning at every bodys house. Lord have mercy on dese here young folks and deliber me from the plantation, I pray.

"Courting dem days wuz like everything I reckon you all do now adays. You promise to 'bey the man, but before you finishing its cussing, Honey.

In olden days husbands loved. Sho God did tend to wife and took care of them and they had to stay home cause it wuz always a new baby. I tell you, Miss Sue, man ought not never had you to find history 'cause you gwine tell it all. As I said, we loved . Is de young folks marrying fur love? Dey don't stay together long enough to warm hands. We went to church together and praised God; led prayer meetings and, yes siree, would feel good.

Now you all done start opening theatres on Sunday. Miss Sue, all dat stuff you putting down will sure make the man laugh.

450004

Interview of Mrs. Marriah Hines - E. Avenue R.F.D. 1.
Oakwood Norfolk, Virginia
By -- David Hoggard
March 26, 1937

APR 14 1937

Mrs. Marriah Hines - Born July 4, 1835, South Hampton County Virginia. a

slave on James Pressmans plantation. Now residing on E. Avenue, Oakwood Norfolk,

Virginia R.F. D. 1.

insert last paragraph to 2

Even though the general course of slavery was cruel, Marriah Hines was

fortunate enough, not to have to endure its severities. James Pressman was one

of the few slave masters that looked upon the slave with a certain degree of com-

passion, to whom Marriah was fortunate, to be owned by. Although slavery in its

self was cruel; but the fact that Mr. Pressman was generous and kind to the slaves

that he owned, because of necessity in the process of his farming, should not be

overlooked. It is quite true that slave masters near him did not grant their slaves

such priviliges as he did. I do not wish to impress the idea that Mr. Pressman did

not approve of slavery, but only his general attitude toward his slaves was different

from the majority of the slaves holders. From the following story of Marriah's life

in slavery, it may be clearly seen that her master was an exception.

Upon interviewing her, she relates her life story as follows -

"I lived with good people, my white folks treated us good. There was plenty of

'em that didn't fare as we did. Some of the poor folks almost starved to death.

Why the way their masters treated them was scandalous, treated them like cats and

dogs. We always had plenty of food, never knowed what it was to want food bad enough

to have to steal it like a whole lot of 'em. Master would always give us plenty

when he give us our rations. Ofcourse we slaves were given food and clothing and

just enough to keep us goin good. Why master would buy cloth by the loads and heaps,

shoes by the big box full; den he'd call us to the house and give each on'us our

share. Plenty to keep us comfortable, course it warn't silk nor satin, no ways the

best there was, but 'twas plenty good 'nough for us, and we was plenty glad to git

[handwritten margin notes:]
seeming similar to Northrup's talk of Ford — extending grace if this is important to the enslaved, how do we represent that?

first employ of animal language

it. When we would look and see how the slaves on the 'jining farm was fareing, 'twould almost make us shed tears. It made us feel like we was gitting 'long most fine. Dat's why we loved 'spected master; 'course he was so good to us.

'Cause master was good and kind to us, some of the other white folks used to call him "nigger lover." He didn't pay dat no mind though. He was a true Christian man, and I mean he sho' lived up to it. He never did force any of us to go to church, if we didn't want to, dat was left to us to 'cide. If you wanted to you could, if you didn't you didn't have to, but he'd always tell us, you ought to go.

Not only was master good but his whole family was too. When the weather was good we worked in the fields and on other little odd jobs that was needed done. We slaves would eat our breakfast, and go to the fields, dare wont no hurry-scurry. Lots o'times when we got in the fields the other slaves had been in the field a long time. Dar was times though we had to git to it early, too, 'pecially if it had been rainy weather and the work had been held up for a day or so. Master didn't make us work a 'tall in bad weather neither when it got real cold. The men might have to git in fire wood or suppin' of that sort but no all day work in the cold - just little odd jobs. We didn't even have to work on Sundays not even in the "house". The master and the preacher both said dat was the Lord's day and you won't spose to work on that day. So we didn't. We'd cook the white folks vittals on Saturday and lots o'times dey eat cold vitals on Sundays. Master would sometimes ask the preacher home to dinner. "You plenty welcome to go home with me for dinner, but you'll have to eat cold vittals 'cause there aint no cooking on Sundays at my house." Lots of times we slaves would take turns on helping 'em serve Sunday meals just 'cause we liked them so much. We hated to see Missie fumbling 'round in the kitchen all out 'a her place. We didn't have to do it, we just did it on our own free will. Master sometimes gives us a little money for it too, which made it all the better. Master and Missus was so good to us we didn't mind working a little on Sundays, in the house. Master had prayer with the whole family every night, prayed for us slaves too. Any of the slaves that wanted to jine him could. Or if they wanted to pray by dem selves they could. Sundays we went to church and stayed the biggest portion of the day. No body had torush home. On our plantation we had general prayer meeting every Wednesday night at church. 'cause some of the masters didn't like the way we slaves carried on we would turn pots down, and tubs to keep the sound from going out. Den we would have a good time, shouting singing and praying just like we pleased. The paddarollers didn't pay us much 'tention coused they knew how master let us do. Dey would say nasty things 'bout master 'cause he let us do like we did.   *paternalism*

We had plenty time to ourselves. Most of the time we spent singing and praying 'cause master was sich a good Christian and most of us had 'fessed religion. Evenings we would spin on the old spinning wheel, quilt make clothes, talk, tell jokes, and a few had learned to weave a little bit from Missus. We would have candy pulls, from cooked molasses, and sing in the moonlight by the tune of an old banjo picker. Challen was mostly seen, not heard, different from youngens of today talking backward and foward cross their mammies and pappies. Challen dat did dat den would git de breath slapped out on 'em. Your mamies didn't have to do it either; any old person would, and send you home to git another lickin'. We slaves had two hours off for dinner, when we could go home and eat before we finished work 'bout sun down. We aint had no colored overseers to whip us nor no white ones. We just went 'long so and did what we had to, wid out no body watching over us. Every body was just plum crazy 'bout master. Doing the day you could see him strutting down the field like a big turkey gobbler to see how the work was going on. Always had a smile and a joke wid you. He allu's tell us we was doing fine, even sometimes when we want. We'd always catch up our work, so he wouldn't have to fuss. We loved Misses and the challen so much we wouldn't even let 'em eat hardly. Missus didn't have to do nothing, hardly. Dare was always some of us round the house.

'Bout a year fore we heard 'bout freedom, master took sick and the slaves   *fear?* wouldn't'er looked sadder if one of their own youngens had been sick. Dey 'spected him to die, and he kept calling for some cabbage. Misses finally let me cook him some cabbage, and let him have some "pot licker" (the water the cabbage was cooked in).

He didn't die den but a few years later he did die. Dat was the first and the last time any cooking ever was done in that house on Sunday.

When master told us we was free it didn't take much 'fect on us. He told us we could go where we pleased and come when we pleased that we didn't have to work for him any more 'less we wanted to. Most of us slaves stayed right there and raised our own crops. Master helped us much as he could. Some of us he gave a cow or a mule or any-thing he could spare to help us. Some of us worked on the same plantation and bought our own little farms and little log cabins, and lived right there till master dies and the family moved away. Some of us lived there right on. Master married me to one of the best colored men in the world, Benjamin F. Hines. I had five chullun by him, four girls and one boy, two of the girls and the boy are dead. Dey died 'bout 1932 or 33 I stay with one a while, den I go and stay a while wid the other one.

We didn't have no public schools in dem days'n time. What little learning you got it from the white chillen."

Marriah is about four feet and a half tall ~~near five feet~~ and weighing about one hundred pounds, ~~with~~ she has a pretty head of white hair covering her round brown face. Her memory of her mother and father is very vague, due to their death when she was young. She is able to dress herself practically with out help, and to get about from place to place alone, enjoying talking about religion and the words ~~what she hears about~~ today.

absence of physical description by interviewers and interviewees alike

Virginia

RL-1

O Terms and phrasing to be checked and verified in further interviews.

31

APR 14 1937

11/26/1937

THE STORY OF "UNCLE" MOBLE HOPSON.
(pronounced Mobile)

Interview Saturday, November 28th at his home on the
Poquoson River.
(Recorded from memory within 1 hour after "being talked to by him")

Uncle Moble hobbles unsteadily from his little shade beside the outhouse into the warm kitchen, leaning heavily on
the arm of his niece. He looks up on hearing my voice, and ex-
tends a gnarled and tobacco-stained hand. He sinks fumblingly
into a chair. It is then that I see that Uncle Moble is blind.

"No, don't mind effen yuh ast me questions. Try tuh answer
'em, I will, best ways I kin. Don't mind et all, effen yuh tell
me whut yuh want to know. Born'd in fifty-two, I was, yessuh,
right her over theer wheer dat grade big elum tree usta be.
Mammy was uh Injun an' muh pappy was uh white man, least-ways
he warn't no slave even effen he was sorta dark-skinned.

*pride in
non-black
father*

"Ole pappy tole me 'bout how cum the whites an' the blacks
an' the Injuns get all mixed up. Way back 'long in dere it war,
be *verrh* new tell me jes' whut year, dey was a tribe uh Injuns livin

'long dis ribber. Dey was kin to de Kink-ko-tans, but dey

wasn't de same. Dey had ober on the James de Kink-ko-tans

an' dey had dis tribe ober here.

"Well, de white man come. Not fum ober dere. De white

man cum cross de Potomac, an' den he cross de York ribber, an' den

he cum on cross de Poquoson ribber into dis place. My pappy

tell me jes' how cum dey cross all uh dose ribbers. He ain't

see it, yuh unnerstand, but he hear tell how et happen.

"Dis whut de white man do. He pick hisself a tall ellum

long side de ribber an' he clamb to de top an' he mark out on

de trunk wid he ax uh section 'long 'bout, oh, 'long 'bout

thirty-fo'ty feet. Den he cut de top off an' den he cut de

bottom off so de thick trunk fall right on de edge uh de ribber.

An' den he hollar out dat ellum log tell he make hisself uh bout

an' he skin off de bark so et don't ketch in de weeds. Den he

make hisse'f uh pattle an' dey all makes pattles an' dey floats

dat boat an' pattles cross to de udder side.

"Well, dey cross de Potomac an' dey has tuh fight de Injuns an'

dey cross de York an' fit some more tell dey kilt all de Injuns or run 'em way. When dey cross de Poquoson dey fine de

Injuns ain't aimin' tuh fight but dey kilt de men an' tek

de Injun women fo' dey wives. Coursen dey warn't no marry-

in' dem at dat time.

"Well dat's how cum my people started. Ah hear tell

on how dey hafta fight de Injuns now an den, an' den de

Britishers come an' dey fit de British.

"An' all uh dat time dere warn't no black blood mixed

in 'em, least wise, not as I heer'd tell uh any. Plenty blacks

'round; an seen 'em. My pappy nevuh would have none. My

oncle had 'em, ober on dat pasture land dere was his land.

"Why I usta get right out dere many uh day and watch 'em
                        in de 'baccy fields.
at work, Big fellars dey was, wid cole-black skins ashinin'

wid sweat jes' lak dey rub hog-fat ober dere faces. Ah ain't

nevuh bothered 'em but my bruther-he daid now sence ninety-three

he got uh hidin' one day fo' goin' in de field wid de blacks.
                                        an ah listen to de grown folk talk on et,
Insert   "Well we all heer tell uh de was, but dey ain't paid so

much mind to et. Tell one day de blacks out in de field an' dey

ain't no one out dere tuh mek 'em work. An' dey stand 'round an' laugh an' dey get down an' wait, but dey don' leave dat

field all de mawning. An' den de word cum dat de Yankees

was a comin,' an' all dem blacks start tuh hoopin' an' holl'rin',

an' den dey go on down to deer snacks an' dey don' do no work

at all dat day.

"An' when de Yanks ^git heer dey ain't none uh de slave-holders

no whers round. Dey all cleared out an' de blacks is singin' an'

prayin' an' shoutin' fo' joy cause *Marse Lincoln done set em

free.

"Well, dey tuk de blacks an' dey march em down de turnpike

to Hampton, an' dey put em tuh work at de fort. Ah ain't nevuh

go ober dere but ah heer tell now de blacks come dere fum all

'round tell dey get so many dey ain't got work fo' 'em tuh do, so

dey put 'em tun pilin' up logs an' teking 'em down agin, an' de

Yankees come and go an' new ones come but dey ain't ^troublin

nothin' much 'ceptin' tuh poach uh hawg or turkey now an' den.

"Ah was jes' a little shaver gittin' in my teens den but ah

remember clear as dey all ah dat. An' ah heer tell of uh tig battle up Bethel way an' dey say dey kilt up dere uh bunch uh

men, de 'federates an' de Yankees both. But ah ain't seed it,

though Oncle Shep Brown done tole me all 'bout et.

"Oncle Shep Brown lived down aways on de ribber. 'Long 'fore

de Yankees come he jined up wid de 'federates. He fit in dat

battle at Big Bethel but he ain't get uh scratch. He tell me

all 'bout de war when he come back home. ~~He tell me all 'bout~~

~~de war when he cum back home.~~ He tell me all 'bout de fall

uh Richmond, he did.

"Was one day down en de lower woods in de shade he tell me

'bout Richmond, oncle Shep did. Why, I remember et jes' lak it

was yestiddy. Was whittlin' uh stick, he was, settin' on uh stump

wid his game laig hunched up on tuh uh bent saplin' He was whitt-

lin' away fo' uh 'long time 'thout sayin' much, an' all at once he

jump up in de air an' de saplin' sprang up an he start in tuh cus-

sin.

"'Gawdammit, gawdammit, gawdammit,' he kept sayin' tuh his-

se'f an' limpin' round on dat laig game wid de romatissum. Ah

know he gonna tell me sompin den cause when Oncle Shep git shcited he always got uh lot tuh say.

"'Gawdammit,' ne say,' 'twas de niggahs tek Richmond,'"

"How dey do dat Uncle Shep?" ah ast, though an knowed he was

gonna tell me anyway.

"'De niggahs done tuk Richmond,'" he kep on sayin' an'

finally he tell me how cum dey tek Richmond.

"'Ah seed et muhse'f,'" he say, "'my comp'ny was stationed

on de turnpike clo. tuh Richmond. We was in uh ole warehouse,'"

he told me, "'wid de winders an' de doors all barred up an'

packed wid ~~tobacey~~ terbacey bales awaitin' fo' ~~de~~ dem Yanks tuh come. An'

we was a-listenin' an' peepin' out an' we been waitin' dere most

all ~~day~~ de ev'nin'. An' den we heer uh whistlin' an' uh roarin' like uh big

blow an' it kep' gittin' closer. But we couldn't see nothin' uh

comin' de night was so dark. ~~But~~ Dat roarin' kept a-gittin' loud-

er an' louder an' 'long 'bout day break there cum fum down de pike

sech uh shoutin' an uh yellin' as nevuh in muh born days ah'd ~~ah had~~

heerd.'

"'An' de men in dat warehouse kept askinkin' away in de

darkness widdout sayin' nothin', cause dey didn't know what

debbils de Yankees was a lettin' loose. But ah a stayed

right there wid dem dat had de courage tuh face et, cause ah

know big noise mean uh little storm.'

   "'Dar was 'bout forty of us left in dat ole warehouse

ahidin' back of dem bales uh cotton an terbaccy, an' peepin out

threw de cracks.'

   "'An' den dey come. Down de street dey come--a shoutin'

an' aprancin' an' a yellin' an' asingin' an' makin' such uh

noise like as ef all hell done been turn't loose. Uh nigguhs.
                                              mob uh

Ah ain't nevub knowed niggubs--even all uh dem niggubs--could

mek sech uh ruckus. One huge sea uh black faces filt de streets

fum wall tuh wall, an' dey wan't nothin' but niggubs in sight.'

   "' Well, suh, dey warn't no usen us firin' on dem cause dey

ain't no way we gonna kill all uh dem niggubs. An pretty soon

dey bus' in de do' uh dat warehouse, an' we stood dere whilst dey

pranced 'rounst us a hoopin' an' holl'rin' an' not techin' us at
                        soljers
all tell de Yankees soldiers cum up, an' tek away our guns, an' mek

us prisoners an' perty soon dey march us intuh town an' lock us
              Libby
up in ole Libby Prison.'

"'Thousings of 'em--den nigguhs.' he say, 'Yassir--was de

nigguhs dat tuk Richmond. Time de Yankees get dere de niggubs

done had ~~already tooken de city.~~'" got de city tuk".

II
Why Uncle Moble is a Negro

Uncle Moble is a noble figure. He turned his head toward

me at my questions, just as straight as if he actually ~~was see-~~
~~ing me.~~ is looking at me

"Yuh wanta know why I'm put with the colored people? ~~when~~
~~my skin is white?~~ Well, ah ain't white an' ah ain't black, least- Sure, ah got white skin, leastwise, was white los' time ah see et.

wise not so fur as ah know. 'Twas the war done that. Fo de

war dere warn't no question come up 'bout et. Ain't been no

schools 'roun' here tuh bothuh 'bout. Blacks work in de fields,

an' de whites ~~run~~ own de fields. Dis land here, been owned by de

Hopson's sence de fust Hopson cum here, i guess, back fo' de

British war, fo' de Injun war, ah reck'n. Ustuh go tuh de

church schoo wid ole Shep Brown's chillun, sat on de same bench,

~~we all~~ ah did.

"But de war changed all dat. Arter de soljers come back home,

it was diff'runt, first dey say dat all whut ain't white, is black.

den
An' ⌄dey tell de Injuns yuh kain't marry no more de whites. An'

den dey tell usen dat we kain't cum no more tuh church school.

An' dey won't let us do no bisness wid de whites, so we is th'own

in wid de blacks.

uh our folk
"Some ⌄moved away, but dey warn't no use uh movin' cause ah

hear tell et be de same ev'y wheer. So perty soon et come time

tuh marry, an' dey ain't no white woman fo' me tuh marry so ah

marries uh black woman. An' dat make me black, ah 'spose 'cause

ah ben livin' black ev'y sence.

"But mah bruther couldn't fine no black woman dat suited

him, ah reckon, cause he married his fust cousin, who was a

Hopson huhse'f.

uh
"Den dere only chile married hisse'f ~~another~~ Hopson, and

Hopsons been marryin' Hopsons ev'y sence, ah reck'n."

"That well out dere? Naw, dat ain't old. Dat ain't been dere mo'un fifteen -

twenty year. De old well, she was ol*though she nevuh war much good. Paw ain't

dug et in de right place. Old Shep Bro n tolt him, but my old man ain't nevuh pay

no mine to old Shep.

But old Shep sho' did know ho uh dig uh well. Ah kin see now him ah comin'

up de lane when paw was adiggin'. Mobile he say - my paw an' me had de same name-

Mobile, ye ain't diggin' dat well de right place.

"Diggin' et wheer ah wants et," ~~announces~~ answers paw, a diggin' away en de hole

shoulder deep.

"Well, ye ain't gonna git much water. O ghta got yo'se'f uh ellum stick."

"Don' need no ellum stick. Diggin' dis well in my own yaad an' ah'm gonna dig

et jes' wheer ah wants et. Go haid an' dig yo' own well."

"ell, old Shep musta got sorta mad, cause he goes home an' de nex' day he

digs hisse'f uh well.

Ah seen him. Ah watched him when he figgered whee r tuh dig dat well. Sho

nuf old Shep got hisse'f uh prime ellum stick fum ahggood sized ~~forked branch.~~ branch dat was forked.

First he skint all de bark off.

"Kain't fine no water lessen ~~de bark skint off,~~ ye skin de bark off," he tell me. "Long 'bout 2-3

feet on each limb, et was. Well, old Shep tek dat ellum stick wid one fork in each hand an' de big end straight up in de air an' he holt it tight an' started

tuhw walk around, wid me followin' right on his heels. An sho' nuff, perty soon

ah seed dat branch commence tuh shake an' den et started tuh bend an' old Shep

le' et lead him across de field wid et bendin' lower all de time tell perty oon

de big end uh dat ellum stick point straight down.

Old Shep marked de spot an' got his pick an' commence tuh dig out dat spot.

An' fo' old Shep had got down mo'un five uh six feet ah be dawg ef he don' hit uh

stream uh water dat filt up de well in uh hurry so dat he git his laigs all wet

fo' he could git out. Kin clamb out.

An' yuh moughten believe et but ah knowed dat tuh be uh fac, cause ah tuk

dat ellum stick in muh own han's an' ah felt dat stick apullin' me back tuh dat

water. No matter which way ah turn, dat stick keep atwistin' me roun' toward dat

water. An' ah tried tuh pull et back an' old Shep tuk holt uh et wid me an' tried

tuh hole et up straight but de big end uh dat ellum branch pult down and pointed

tuh dat well spite uh both uh us."

"Still dere? Nawsuh, ah reckon date old well been crumbled in an' filledp

long time now. Old Shep died back en 93, ah reckon. His old shack blowed down, an'

ah reckon dat ole well all covered up. But dat was some well while she lasted.

Gave mo' water dan all de udder wells in Poquoson, ah reckon.

Jones, Albert

APR 14 1937

42

Interview of Ex-slave and
Civil War Veteran
<u>Portsmouth, Virginia</u>
By -- Thelma Dunston
January 8, 1937

Civil War Veteran of Portsmouth, Virginia

On the out skirts of Portsmouth, Virginia, where one seldom hears of or goes
for sight seeing lives Mr. Albert Jones. In a four room cottage at 726 Lindsey
Avenue, the aged Civil War Veteran lives alone with the care of Mr. Jones' niece,
who resides next door to him. He has managed to survive his ninety-fifth year.
It is almost a miracle to see a man at his age as suple as he.

On entering a scanty room in the small house, Mr. Jones was nodding in a
chair near the stove. When asked about his early life, he straightened up on his
spine, crossed his legs and said, "I's perty old - ninety six. I was born a slave
in Souf Hampton county, but my mastah wuz mighty good to me. He won't ruff; dat is
'f yer done right."

The aged man cleared his throat and chuckled. Then he said, "But you better
never let mastah catch yer wif a book or paper, and yer couldn't praise God so he
could hear yer. If yer done dem things, he sho' would beat yer. 'Course he wuz good
to me, 'cause I never done none of 'em. My work won't hard neiver. I had to wait on
my mastah, open de gates fer him, drive de wagon and tend de horses. I was sort of
a house boy."

"Fer twenty years I stayed wif mastah, and I didn't try to run away. When I
wuz twenty one, me and one of my brothers run away to fight wif the Yankees. Us left
Souf Hampton county and went to Petersburg. Dere we got some food. Den us went to
Fort Hatton where we met some more slaves who had done run away. When we got in Fort
Hatton, us had to cross a bridge to git to de Yankees. De rebels had torn de bridge
down. We all got together and builded back de bridge, and we went on to de Yankees.
Dey give us food and clothes.

The old man then got up and emptied his mouth of the tobacco juice, scratched his bald head and continued. "Yer know, I was one of de first colored cavalry soljers, and I fought in Company "K". I fought for three years and a half. Sometimes I slept out doors, and sometimes I slept in a tent. De Yankees always give us plenty of blankets."

"During the war some un us had to always stay up nights and watch fer de rebels. Plenty of nights I has watched, but de rebels never 'tacked us when I wuz on."

"Not only wuz dere men slaves dat run to de Yankees, but some un de women slaves followed dere husbands. Dey use to help by washing and cooking."

"One day when I wuz fighting, de rebels shot at me, and dey sent a bullet through my hand. I wuz lucky not to be kilt. Look! See how my hand is?"

The old man held up his right hand, and it was half closed. Due to the wound he received in the war, that was as far as he could open his hand.

Still looking at his hand Mr. Jones said, "But dat didn't stop me, I had it bandaged and kept on fighting."

"The uniform dat I wore wuz blue wif brass buttons; a blue cape, lined wif red flannel, black leather boots and a blue cap. I rode on a bay color horse - fact every body in Company "K" had bay color horses. I tooked my knap-sack and blankets on de horse back. In my knap-sack I had water, hard tacks and other food."

"When de war ended, I goes back to my mastah and he treated me like his brother. Guess he wuz scared of me 'cause I had so much ammunition on me. My brother, who went wif me to de Yankees, caught rheumatism doing de war. He died after de war ended."

Tolls · C. More

Virginia
1938-9

FOLKLORE

Material from Upper Guinea.

In the upper part of Guinea, generally, known as the "Hook," you will find two very interesting characters, both Negroes. Aunt Susan Kelly, who is a ~~hundred~~ years old, and Simon Stokes, who is near a hundred.

Aunt Susan is loved by all who know her, for she is a very lovable old Negro.

Aunt Susan's Story

"My mammy, Anna Burrell, wuz a slave, her massa wuz Col. Hayes, of Woodwell; he wuz very good ter his slaves. He nebber sold mammy or us chilluns; he kept we alls tergether, and we libed in a little cabin in de yard.

"My job wuz mindin' massa's and missus' chilluns all dey long, and puttin' dem ter baid at night; dey had ter habe a story told ter dem befo' dey would go ter sleep; and de baby hed ter be rocked; and I had ter sing fo' her 'Rock a-by baby, close dem eyes, befo' ole san man comes, rock a-by baby don' let old san man cotch yo' peepin'; befo' she would go ter sleep.

"Mammy used ter bake ash-cakes; dey wuz made wid meal, wid a little salt and mixed wid water; den mammy would rake up de ashes in de fire-place; den she would make up de meal in round cakes, and put dem on de hot bricks ter bake; wen dey hed cooked roun' de edges, she would put ashes on de top ob dem, and wen dey wuz nice and brown she took dem out and washed dem off wid water.

"Mammy said it wuz very bad luck ter meet a woman early in de mornin' walkin'; and nebber carry back salt dat yo' habe borrowed, fo' it will bring bad luck ter yo' and ter de one yo' brung it ter. If yo' nose iches on de right side a man is comin', if de lef' side iches a woman is comin'; if it iches on de end a man and woman is sho' ter come in a short.

"For a hawk ter fly ober de house is sho' sign ob death, fo' de hawk will call corpses wen he flies ober."

what qualities as 'good' and how do we talk about it?

Simon Stokes, son of Kit and Anna Stokes, is quite a type. He and his
parents ~~without~~ with his brothers and sisters were slaves; owned by George W. Billups,
of Mathews County, who later moved to Gloucester County and bought a farm near
Gloucester Point. They had eleven children, Simon is the only one living.

Simon's Story

"Massa George and missus wuz good ter his slaves. My mammy wuz missus'
cook; and him and de odder boys on de farm worked in de co'n and de terbaccer
and cotton fields.

"Me sho' didn't like dat job, pickin' worms off de terbaccer plants; fo' our
oberseer wuz de meanes old hound you'se eber seen, he hed hawk eyes fer seein'
de worms on de terbaccer, so yo' sho' hed ter git dem all, or you'd habe ter bite
all de worms dat yo' miss into, ot git three lashes on yo' back wid his old
lash, and dat wuz powfull bad, wusser dan bittin' de worms, fer yo' could bite
right smart quick, and dat wuz all dat dar wuz ter it; but dem lashes done last
a pow'full long time.

"Me sho' did like ter git behind de ox-team in de co'n field, fo' I could
sing and holler all de day, "Gee thar Buck, whoa thar Peter, git off dat air
co'n, what's de matter wid yo' Buck, can't yo hear, gee thar Buck.

" In de fall wen de simmons wuz ripe, me and de odder boys sho' had a big
time possum huntin', we alls would git two or three a night; and we alls would
put dem up and feed dem hoe-cake and simmons ter git dem nice and fat; den my
mammy would roast dem wid sweet taters round them. Dey wuz sho' good, all
roasted nice and brown wid de sweet taters in de graby.

"We alls believed dat it wuz bad luck ter turn back if yer started anywher,
if yo' did bad luck would sho' foller yer; but ter turn yo' luck, go back and
make a cross in yo' path and spit in it."

450001

Autobiography of Richard Slaughter

(Given by himself as an oral account during an interview between himself
and writer, December 27, 1936.) Claude W. Anderson -- Hampton, Virginia

"Come in, son. Have a seat, who are you and how are you? My life?
Oh! certainly you don't want to hear that! Well, son, have you been
born again? Do you know Christ? Well, that's good. Good for you. Amen.
I'M glad to hear it. Always glad to talk to any true Christian liver.
God bless you, son.

"I was born January 9, 1849 on the James at a place called Epps
Island, City Point. I was born a slave. How old am I ! Well, there's the
date. Count it up for yourself. My owner's name was Dr. Richard B. Epps.
I stayed there until I was around thirteen or fourteen years old when I
came to Hampton.

"I don't know much about the meanness of slavery. There was so
many degrees in slavery, and I belonged to a very nice man. He never
sold but one man, fur's I can remember, and that was cousin Ben. Sold
him South. Yes. My master was a nice old man. He ain't living now. Dr.
Epps died and his son wrote me my age. I got it upstairs in a letter now.

"It happened this a-way. Hampton was already burnt when I came here.
I came to Hampton in June 1862. The Yankees burned Hampton and the fleet
went up the James River. My father and mother and cousins went aboard
the Meritansa with me. You see, my father and three or four men left
in the darkness first and got aboard. The gun boats would fire on the
towns and plantations and run the white folks off. After that they would
carry all the colored folks back down here to Old Point and put 'em
behind the Union lines. I know the names of all the gunboats that came
up the river. Yessir. There was the Galena, we called her the old cheese
box, the Delware, the Yankee, the Mosker, and the Meritansa which was
the ship I was board of. That same year the Merrimac and Monitor fought off

Newport News Point. No, I didn't see it. I didn't come down all the way on the
gunboat. I had the measles on the Meritanza and was put off at Harrison's Land-
ing. When McClelland retreated from Richmond through the peninsula to Washington,
I came to Hampton as a government water boy.

"While I was aboard the gunboat, she captured a rebel gunboat at a
place called Drury's Bluff. When I first came to Hampton, there were only
barracks where the Institute is; when I returned General Armstrong had done
rite smart.

"I left Hampton still working as a water boy and went to Quire Creek, Bell
Plains, Va., a place near Harper's Ferry. I left the creek aboard a steamer, the
General Hooker, and went to Alexandria, Va. Abraham Lincoln came aboard the
steamer and we carried him to Mt. Vernon, George Washington's old home. What did
he look like? Why, he looked more like an old preacher than anything I know.
Heh! Heh! Heh! Have you ever seen any pictures of him? Well, if you seen a picture
of him, you seen him. He's just like the picture.

"You say you think I speak very good English. Heh! Heh! Heh! Well, son
I ought to. I been everywhere. No I never went to what you would call school
except to school as a soldier. I went to Baltimore in 1864 and enlisted. I was
about 17 years old then. My officers' names were Capt. Joe Reed, Lieutenant
Stimson, and Colonel Joseph E. Perkins. I was assigned to the Nineteenth Regiment of Maryland Company B. While I was in training, they fought at Petersburg.
I went to the regiment in '64 and stayed in until '67. I was a cook. They
taken Richmond the fifth day of April 1865. On that day I walked up the road
in Richmond.

"When we left Richmond, my brigade was ordered to Brownsville, Texas.
We went there by way of Old Point Comfort, where we went aboard a transport.
When we got to Brownsville, I was detailed to a hospital staff. We arrived
in Brownsville in January 1867. The only thing that happened in Brownsville

while I was there was the hanging of three Mexicans for the murder of an
aide. In September we left Brownsville and came back to Baltimore. Before
we left I was sent up the Rio Grande to Ringo Barracks as boss cook.

"I then returned to Hampton and lived as an oysterman and fisherman
for over forty years.

"I have never been wounded. My clothes have been cut off me by
bullets but the Lord kept them off my back, I guess.

"I tell you what I did once. My cousin and I went down to the shore
once. The river shore, you know, up where I was born. While we were walking
along catching tadpoles, minnows, and anything we could catch, I happened to
see a big moccasin snake hanging in a sumac bush just a swinging his head back
and forth. I swung at 'im with a stick and he swelled his head all up big and
rared back. Then I hit 'im and knocked him on the ground flat. His belly was
very big so we kept hittin' 'im on it until he opened his mouth and a cat-
fish as long as my arm (forearm), jumped out jest a flopping. Well the cat-
fish had a big belly too, so we beat 'em on his belly until he opened his
mouth and out came one of these women's snapper pocketbooks. You know the
kind that closes by a snap at the top. Well the pocket book was swelling all
out, so we opened it, and guess what was in it? Two big copper pennies. I
gave my cousin one and I took one. Now you mayn't believe that, but it's true.
I been trying to make people believe that for near fifty years. You can put
it in the book or not, jest as you please, but it's true. That fish swallowed
some woman's pocketbook and that snake just swallowed him. I have told men
that for years and they wouldn't believe me.

"While I was away my father died in Hampton. He waited on an officer.
My mother lived in Hampton and saw me married in 1874. I bought a lot on Union
Street for a hundred dollars cash. I reared a nephew, gave him the lot and the
house I built on it an he threw it away. When I moved around here, I paid

cash for this home.

"Did slaves ever run away! Lord yes. All the time. Where I was born, there is a lots of water. Why there used to be as high as ten and twelve Dutch three masters in the habor at a time. I used to catch little snakes and other things like terapins and sell 'em to the sailor for to eat roaches on the ships. In those days a good captain would hide a slave way up in the top sail and carry him out of Virginia to New York and Boston.

"I never went in the Spanish American War. Too old, but I had some cousins that enlisted. That was during McKinley's time He went down the Texas and some of them other ships they gave Puerto Rico Hail Columbia. They blew up the Maine with a mine. She was blowed up inward. The Maine left Hampton Roads going towards Savannah. Then they looked at what was left of her all the steel was bent inward which shows that she was blowed up from the out- side in. Understand. During the World War I went to Washington and haven't been anyplace since. I'm a little hard of hearing and have high blood pressure. So I have to sit most the time. Got an invitation in there now wantin' me to come to a grand reunion of Yankees and the Rebels this year but I can't go. Getting too old. Well goodbye, son. Glad to have you come again sometime."

Autobiography of Elizabeth Sparks

(Interviewed at Matthews Court House, Virginia January 13, 1937 By Claude W. Anderson.)

Come in boys. Sure am glad ter see ya. You're lookin' so well. That's whut I say. Fight boys! Hold em! You're doin' alright. Me, I 'm so mean nothin' can hurt me. What's that! You want me to tell yer 'bout slavery days. Well I kin tell yer, but I ain't. S'all past now; so I say let 'er rest 's too awful to tell anyway. yer're too young to know all that talk anyway. 'ell I'll tell yer some to put in yer book, but I ain'ta goin' tell yer the worse.

My mistress's name was Miss Jennie Brown. No, I guess I'd better not tell yer. Done forgot about dat. Oh well, I'll tell yer. Some, I guess. She died 'bout four years ago. Bless her. She 'uz a good woman. Course I mean she'd slap an' beat yer once in a while but she warn't no woman fur fighting fussin' an' beatin' yer all day lak some I know. She was too young when da war ended fur that. Course no while folks perfect. Her parents a little rough, Whut dat? Kin I tell yer about her parents? Lord yes! I wasn't born then but my parents told me. But I ain't a goin' tell yer nuffin. No I ain't. Tain't no sense fur yer ta know 'bout all those mean white folks. Dey all daid now. They meany good I reckon. Leastways most of 'em got salvation on their death beds.

Well I'll tell yer some, but I ain'ta goin' tell yer much more. No sir. Shep Miller was my master. His ol' father , he was a tough one. Lord! I've seen 'im kill 'em. He'd git the meanest overseers to put over 'em. Why I member time after he was dead when I'd peep in the closet an' jes' see his old clothes hangin' there an' jes' fly. Yessir, I'd run from them clothes an' I was jes' a little girl then. He wuz that way with them black folks. Is he in heaven! No, he ain't in heaven! Went past heaven. He was clerk an' was he tough! Sometimes he beat 'em until they couldn't work. Give 'em more work than they could do. They'd git beatin' if they didn't get work done. Bought my mother, a little girl, when he was married. She wuz a real Christian an' he respected her a little. Didn't beat her so much. Course he beat her once in a

while. Shep Miller was terrible. There was no end to the beatin' I saw it wif
my own eyes.

Beat women! Why sure he beat women. Beat women jes' lak men. Beat women
naked an' wash 'em down in brine, Some times they beat 'em so bad, they jes'
couldn't stand it an' they run away to the woods. If yer git in the woods, they
couldn't git yer. Yer could hide an' people slip yer somepin' to eat. Then he
call yer every day. After while he tell one of colored foreman tell yer come on
back. He ain'ta goin' beat yer anymore. They had colored foreman but they always
have a white overseer. Foreman git yer to come back an' then he beat yer to death
again.

They worked six days fum sun to sun. If they forcin' wheat or other crops,
they start to work long 'fo day. Usual work day began when the horn blew an' stop
when the horn blew. They git off jes' long 'nuf to eat at noon. Didn't have much
to eat. They git some suet an' slice a bread fo' breakfas, Well, they give the
colored people an allowance every week. Fo' dinner they'd eat ash cake baked on
blade of a hoe.

I lived at Seaford then an' was roun' fifteen or sixteen when my mistress
married. Shep Miller lived at Springdale. I 'member jes' as well when they gave me
to Jennie. We wuz all in a room helpin' her dress. She was soon to be married, an'
she turns 'roun an' sez to us. Which of yer niggers think I'm gonna git when I
git married? We all say,'I doan know,' An' she looks right at me an' point her
finger at me like this an' sayed 'yer!' I was so glad. I had to make 'er believe
I 'us cryin', but I was glad to go with 'er. She didn't beat. She wuz jes' a
young thing. Course she take a whack at me sometime, but that weren't nuffin'.
Her mother was a mean ol' thin'. She'd beat yer with a broom or a leather strap
or anythin' she'd git her hands on.

She uster make my aunt Caroline knit all day an' when she git so tired
aftah dark that she'd git sleepy, she'd make 'er stan' up an knit. She work her
so hard that she'd go to sleep standin' up an' every time her haid nod an' her

women's work overseen by women

knees sag, the lady'd come down across her haid with a switch. That wuz Miss

Jennie's mother. She'd give the cook jes' so much meal to make bread fum an'
effen she burnt it, she'd be scared to death cause they'd whup her. I 'member
plenty of times the cook ask say. 'Marsa please 'scuse dis bread, hits a little
too brown. 'Yessir! Beat the devil out 'er if she burn dat bread.

I went wif Miss Jennie an' worked at house. I didn't have to cook. I got
permission to git married. Yer always had to git permission. White folks 'ud
give yer away. Yer jump cross a broom stick tergether an' yer wuz married. My
husband' lived on another plantation. I slep' in my mistress's room but I ain't
slep' in any bed. Nosir! I slep' on a carpet, an' ole rug, befo' the fiahplace.
I had to git permission to go to church, everybody did. We c'ud set in the
gallery at the white folks service in the mornin' an' in the evenin' the folk
held baptise service in the gallery wif white present.

Shep went to war but not for long. We didn't see none of it, but the
slaves knew what the war wuz 'bout. After the war they tried to fool the slaves
'bout freedom an' wanted to keep 'em on a workin' but the Yankees told 'em they
wuz free. They sent some of the slaves to South Carolina, when the Yankees came
near to keep the Yankees from gittin' 'em. Sent cousin James to South Carolina.
I nevah will forgit when the Yankees came through. They wuz takin' all the live-
stock an' all the men slaves back to Norfolk, wid 'em to break up the system. White
folks head wuz jes' goin' to keep on havin' slaves. The slaves wanted freedom, but
they's scared to tell the white folks so. Anyway the Yankees wuz givin' everythin'
to the slaves. I kin heah 'am tellin' ol' Missy now. Yes! give'er clothes. Let'er
take anythin' she wants. They even took some of Miss Jennie's things an' offered
'em to me. I didn't take 'em tho' cause she'd been purty nice to me. Whut tickled
me wuz my husban', John Sparks. He didn't want to leave me an' go cause he didn't
know whah they's takin' 'em nor what they's gonna do, but he wanted to be free;
so he played lame to keep fum goin'. He was jes' a limpin' 'round. It was all I

could do to keep fum laffin'. I kin hear MissJennie now yellin' at them Yankees. No! who are yer to judge. I'll be the judge. If John Sparks wants to stay here, he'll stay, they was gonna take 'im anyhow an' he went inside to pack an' the baby started cryin'. So one of 'em said that as long as he had a wife an' a baby that young they guess he could stay. They took all the horses, cows, and pigs and chickens an' anything they could use an' left. I was about nineteen when I married. I wuz married in 1861, my oldest boy was born in 1862 an' the fallin' of Richmond came in 1865.

Before Miss Jennie was married she was born an' lived at her old home right up the river heah. Yer kin see the place fum ou side heah.On the plantation my mother wuz a house woman. She had to wash white folks clothes all day an' huh's after dark. Sometimes she'd be washin' clothes way up 'round midnight. Nosir, couldn't wash any nigguh's clothes in daytime. My mother lived in a big one room log house wif an' upstairs. Sometimes the white folks give yer 'bout ten cents to spend. A woman with children 'ud git 'bout half bushel of meal a week; a childless woman 'ud git 'bout a peck an' a half of meal a week. If yer wuz workin', they'd give yer shoes. Children went barefooted, the yeah 'round. The men on the road got one cotton shirt an' jacket. I had five sisters an' five brothers. Might as well quit lookin' ah me. I ain't gonna tell yer any more. Cain't tell yer all I know. Ol Shep might come back an' git me. hy if I was to tell yer the really bad things, some of dem daid white folks would come right up outen dere graves. Well, I'll tell somemore, but I cain't tell all.

Once in a while they was free nigguhs come fum somewhah. They could come see yer if yer was their folks. Nigguhs used to go way off in quarters an' slip an' have meetins. They called it stealin' the meetin'. The children used to teach me to read. Schools! Son, there warn't no schools for niggers. Slaves went to bed when they didn't have anything to do. Most time they went to bed when they could. Sometimes the men had to shuck corn till eleven and twelve o'clock at night.

If you went out at night the paddyrols 'ud catch yer if yer was out aftah time without a pass. Mos' a the slaves was afeared to go out.

Plenty of slaves ran away. If they ketch 'em they beat 'em near to death.

But yer know dey's good an' bad people every where. That's the way the white folks wuz. Some had hearts; some had gizzards 'stead o' hearts.

When my mothers's master died, he called my mother an' brother Major an' got religion an' talked so purty. He say he so sorry that he hadn't found the Lord before an' had nuttin' gainst his colored people. He was sorry an' scared, but confessed. My mother died twenty years since then at the age of seventy-fo'. She wuz very religious an' all wite folks set store to 'er.

Old Massa done so much wrongness I couldn't tell yer all of it. Slave girl Betty Lilly always had good clothes an' all the priviliges. She wuz a favorite of his'n. But cain't tell all! God's got all! We uster sing a song when he was shippin' the slaves to sell 'em 'bout "Massa's Gwyne Sell Us Termerrer." No, I cain't sing it for yer. My husban' lived on the plantation nex' to my mistress. He lived with a bachelor master. He tell us say once when he was a pickinnany ol' Marse Williams shot at 'im. He didn't shoot 'em; he jes' shoot in the air an' ol' man wuz so sceared he ran home an' got in his mammy's bed. Massa Williams uster play wif 'em; then dey got so bad that they'ud run an' grab 'is laige so's he couldn't hardly walk so when he sees 'em he jes' shoots in de air. Ol' Massa, he, jes' come on up ter the cabin an' say "mammy whah dat boy?" She say, in dah undah the bed. Yer done scared 'im to deaf! Ol' Massa go on in an' say, Boy! What's the mattah wid yer. Boy say, yer shot me master yer shot me! Master say, Aw Gwan! -- Git up an' come along. I ain't shot yer. I jes' shot an' scared yer. Heh! Heh! Heh! Yessir my ol' husban' sayed he sure was scared that day.

Now yer take dat an' go. Put that in the book. Yer kin make out wif dat. I ain't a gonna tell yer no more. Nosir. The end a time is at hand anyway. 'Tain't no use ter write a book. The Bible say when it git so's yer cain't tell one season from t'other the worl's comin' to end; here hit is so warm in winter that feels like summer. Goodbye. Keep lookin' good an' come again.

NEGRO PIONEER TEACHER OF PORTSMOUTH, VIRGINIA

D - 5

APR 14 1937

55

450002

APR 26 1937

One of the rooms in the Old Folks Home for Colored in Portsmouth, Virginia is occupied by an ex-slave -- one of the first Negro teachers of Portsmouth.

On meeting Miss Mary Jane Wilson, very little questioning was needed to get her to tell of her life. Drawing her chair near a small stove, she said, "my Mother and Father was slaves, and when I was born, that made me a slave. I was the only child. My Mother was owned by one family, and my Father was owned by another family. My mother and father was allowed to live together. One day my father's mastah took my father to Norfolk and put him in a jail to stay until he could sell him. My missus bought my father so he could be with us."

"During this time I was small, and I didn't have so much work to do. I jus helped around the house."

"I was in the yard one day, and I saw so many men come marching down the street, I ran and told my mother what I'd seen. She tried to tell me what it was all about, but I couldn't understand her. Not long after that we was free."

Taking a long breath, the old woman said, "My father went to work in the Norfolk Navy Yard as a teamster. He began right away buying us a home. We was one of the first Negro land owners in Portsmouth after emancipation. My father builed his own house. It's only two blocks from here, and it still stands with few improvements."

With a broad smile Miss Wilson added, "I didn't get any teachings when I was a slave. When I was free, I went to school. The first school I went to was held in a church. Soon they builded a school building that was called, 'Chestnut Street Academy', and I went there. After finishing Chestnut Street Academy, I went to Hampton Institute. In 1874, six years after Hampton Institute was started, I graduated."

This collection of slave narratives had its beginning in the second year of the former Federal Writers' Project (now the Writers' Program), 1936, when several state Writers' Projects-- notably those of Florida, Georgia, and South Carolina--recorded interviews with ex-slaves residing in those states. On April 22, 1937, a standard questionnaire for field workers drawn up by John A. Lomax, then National Advisor on Folklore and Folkways for the Federal Writers' Project,[1] was issued from Washington as "Supplementary Instructions #9-E to The American Guide Manual" (appended below). Also associated with the direction and criticism of the work in the Washington office of the Federal Writers' Project were Henry G. Alsberg, Director; George Cronyn, Associate Director; Sterling A. Brown, Editor on Negro Affairs; Mary Lloyd, Editor; and B. A. Botkin, Folklore Editor succeeding Mr. Lomax.[2]

---

[1] Mr. Lomax served from June 25, 1936, to October 23, 1937, with a ninety-day furlough beginning July 24, 1937. According to a memorandum written by Mr. Alsberg on March 23, 1937, Mr. Lomax was "in charge of the collection of folklore all over the United States for the Writers' Project. In connection with this work he is making recordings of Negro songs and cowboy ballads. Though technically on the payroll of the Survey of Historical Records, his work is done for the Writers and the results will make several national volumes of folklore. The essays in the State Guides devoted to folklore are also under his supervision." Since 1933 Mr. Lomax has been Honorary Curator of the Archive of American Folk Song, Library of Congress.

[2] Folklore Consultant, from May 2 to July 31, 1938; Folklore Editor, from August 1, 1938, to August 31, 1939.

On August 31, 1939, the Federal Writers' Project became the Writers' Program, and the National Technical Project in Washington was terminated. On October 17, the first Library of Congress Project, under the sponsorship of the Library of Congress, was set up by the Work Projects Administration in the District of Columbia, to continue some of the functions of the National Technical Project, chiefly those concerned with books of a regional or nation-wide scope. On February 12, 1940, the project was reorganized along strictly conservation lines, and on August 16 it was succeeded by the present Library of Congress Project (Official Project No. 165-2-26-7, Work Project No. 540).

The present Library of Congress Project, under the sponsorship of the Library of Congress, is a unit of the Public Activities Program of the Community Service Programs of the Work Projects Administration for the District of Columbia. According to the Project Proposal (WPA Form 301), the purpose of the Project is to "collect, check, edit, index, and otherwise prepare for use WPA records, Professional and Service Projects."

The Writers' Unit of the Library of Congress Project processes material left over from or not needed for publication by the state Writers' Projects. On file in the Washington office in August, 1939, was a large body of slave narratives, photographs of former slaves, interviews with white informants regarding slavery, transcripts of laws, advertisements, records of sale,

transfer, and manumission of slaves, and other documents. As un-
published manuscripts of the Federal Writers' Project these
records passed into the hands of the Library of Congress Project
for processing; and from them has been assembled the present collection of some two thousand narratives from the following seventeen states: Alabama, Arkansas, Florida, Georgia, Indiana, Kansas,
Kentucky, Maryland, Mississippi, Missouri, North Carolina, Ohio,
Oklahoma, South Carolina, Tennessee, Texas, and Virginia.[1]

The work of the Writers' Unit in preparing the narratives for
deposit in the Library of Congress consisted principally of ar-
ranging the manuscripts and photographs by states and alphabeti-
cally by informants within the states, listing the informants and
illustrations, and collating the contents in seventeen volumes
divided into thirty-three parts. The following material has been
omitted: Most of the interviews with informants born too late to
remember anything of significance regarding slavery or concerned
chiefly with folklore; a few negligible fragments and unidentified
manuscripts; a group of Tennessee interviews showing evidence

---

[1] The bulk of the Virginia narratives is still in the state of-
fice. Excerpts from these are included in The Negro in Virginia,
compiled by Workers of the Writers' Program of the Work Projects
Administration in the State of Virginia, Sponsored by the Hampton
Institute, Hastings House, Publishers, New York, 1940. Other
slave narratives are published in Drums and Shadows, Survival
Studies among the Georgia Coastal Negroes, Savannah Unit, Georgia
Writers' Project, Work Projects Administration, University of
Georgia Press, 1940. A composite article, "Slaves," based on ex-
cerpts from three interviews, was contributed by Elizabeth Lomax
to the American Stuff issue of Direction, Vol. 1, No. 3, 1938.

of plagiarism; and the supplementary material gathered in connection with the narratives. In the course of the preparation of these volumes, the Writers' Unit compiled data for an essay on the narratives and partially completed an index and a glossary. Enough additional material is being received from the state Writers' Projects, as part of their surplus, to make a supplement, which, it is hoped, will contain several states not here represented, such as Louisiana.

All editing had previously been done in the states or the Washington office. Some of the pencilled comments have been identified as those of John A. Lomax and Alan Lomax, who also read the manuscripts. In a few cases, two drafts or versions of the same interview have been included for comparison of interesting variations or alterations.

II

Set beside the work of formal historians, social scientists, and novelists, slave autobiographies, and contemporary records of abolitionists and planters, these life histories, taken down as far as possible in the narrators' words, constitute an invaluable body of unconscious evidence or indirect source material, which scholars and writers dealing with the South, especially social psychologists and cultural anthropologists, cannot afford to reckon without. For the first and the last time, a large number of surviving slaves (many of whom have since died) have been permitted to tell their own story, in their own

way. In spite of obvious limitations--bias and fallibility of
both informants and interviewers, the use of leading questions,
unskilled techniques, and insufficient controls and checks--
this saga must remain the most authentic and colorful source
of our knowledge of the lives and thoughts of thousands of slaves,
of their attitudes toward one another, toward their masters,
mistresses, and overseers, toward poor whites, North and South,
the Civil War, Emancipation, Reconstruction, religion, education,
and virtually every phase of Negro life in the South.

The narratives belong to folk history--history recovered from
the memories and lips of participants or eye-witnesses, who
mingle group with individual experience and both with observation,
hearsay, and tradition. Whether the narrators relate what they
actually saw and thought and felt, what they imagine, or what
they have thought and felt about slavery since, now we know <u>why</u>
they thought and felt as they did. To the white myth of slavery
must be added the slaves' own folklore and folk-say of slavery.
The patterns they reveal are folk and regional patterns--the patterns of field hand, house and body servant, and artisan; the
patterns of kind and cruel master or mistress; the patterns of
Southeast and Southwest, lowland and upland, tidewater and inland,
smaller and larger plantations, and racial mixture (including Cre-
ole and Indian).

The narratives belong also to folk literature. Rich not only
in folk songs, folk tales, and folk speech but also in folk hu-
mor and poetry, crude or skilful in dialect, uneven in tone and

treatment, they constantly reward one with earthy imagery, salty phrase, and sensitive detail. In their unconscious art, exhibited in many a fine and powerful short story, they are a contribution to the realistic writing of the Negro. Beneath all the surface contradictions and exaggerations, the fantasy and flattery, they possess an essential truth and humanity which surpasses as it supplements history and literature.

Washington, D. C.   B. A. Botkin
June 12, 1941   Chief Editor, Writers' Unit
                                     Library of Congress Project

SELECTED RECORDS

Bearing on the History of the Slave Narratives

From the correspondence and memoranda files of the Washington
office of the Federal Writers' Project the following instructions and criticisms relative to the slave narrative collection,
issued from April 1 to September 8, 1937, have been selected.
They throw light on the progress of the work, the development
of materials and methods, and some of the problems encountered.

1. Copy of Memorandum from George Cronyn to Mrs. Eudora R.
    Richardson. April 1, 1937.

2. Autograph Memorandum from John A. Lomax to George Cronyn.
    April 9, 1937.

3. Copy of Memorandum from George Cronyn to Edwin Bjorkman,
    enclosing a Memorandum from John A. Lomax on "Negro Dialect
    Suggestions." April 14, 1937.

4. Mimeographed "Supplementary Instructions #9-E to the Ameri-
    can Guide Manual. Folklore. Stories from Ex-Slaves."
    April 22, 1937. Prepared by John A. Lomax.

5. Copy of Memorandum from George Cronyn to Edwin Bjorkman.
    May 3, 1937.

6. Copy of Memorandum from Henry G. Alsberg to State Directors
    of the Federal Writers' Project. June 9, 1937.

7. Copy of "Notes by an Editor on Dialect Usage in Accounts by
    Interviews with Ex-Slaves." June 20, 1937. Prepared by
    Sterling A. Brown.

8. Copy of Memorandum from Henry G. Alsberg to State Directors
    of the Federal Writers' Project. July 30, 1937.

9. Copy of Memorandum from Henry G. Alsberg to State Directors
    of the Federal Writers' Project. September 8, 1937.

Sent to: NORTH & SOUTH CAROLINA, GEORGIA, ALABAMA
LOUISIANA, TEXAS, ARKANSAS, TENNESSEE,
KENTUCKY, MISSOURI, MISSISSIPPI, OKLA.

April 1, 1937

Mrs. Eudora R. Richardson, Acting State Director
Federal Writers' Project, WPA
Rooms 321-4, American Bank Building
Richmond, Virginia

Subj: Folklore

Dear Mrs. Richardson:

We have received from Florida a remarkably interesting collection of autobiographical stories by ex-slaves. Such
documentary records by the survivors of a historic period in
America are invaluable, both to the student of history and to
creative writers.

If a volume of such importance can be assembled we
will endeavor to secure its publication. There undoubtedly
is material of this sort to be found in your State by making
the proper contact through tactful interviewers. While it is
desirable to give a running story of the life of each subject,
the color and human interest will be greatly enhanced if it is
told largely in the words of the person interviewed. The peculiar idiom is often more expressive than a literary account.

We shall be very glad to know if you have undertaken
any research of this sort, or plan to do so.

Very truly yours,

George Cronyn
Associate Director
Federal Writers' Project

GWCronyn/a

4/9/1937

Mr. Cronyn:

In replying to this letter I would like for you to _____ _____ especially two stories:

1. _Lula Flannigan_ by Sarah H. Hall
   Athens, Ga.

2. _Uncle Willis_, Miss Velma Bell,
   Supervisor, Athens, Ga.

___ the stories are worth while but these two are especially (one entirely) in dialect and abound in human interest _____. All the interviews should ___ by the Negro expressions I much prefer to read ____

edited (but typed) "interviews", and I
should like to see as soon
as possible all the ...... for
to .... Miss Dixon before...

It is most important,
too, to secure copies of "...
...., ... and the
like." This item is new and
all the states should send
in similar material.

Yours,

(Transcript of Preceding Autograph Memorandum)

4/9/37

Mr. Cronyn:

In replying to this letter I should like for you to commend especially two stories:

1. Lula Flannigan by Sarah H. Hall Athens, Ga.

2. Uncle Willis, Miss Velma Bell, Supervisor, Athens, Ga.

All the stories are worth while but these two are mainly (one entirely) in dialect and abound in human interest touches. All the interviewers should copy the Negro expressions.

I much prefer to read unedited (but typed) "interviews," and I should like to see as soon as possible all the seventy-five to which Miss Dillard refers.

It is most important, too, to secure copies of "slave codes, overseers codes and the like." This item is new and all the states should send in similar material.

Yours,

John A. Lomax

Sent to: North and South Carolina, Georgia,
Alabama, Louisiana, Texas, Arkansas,
Tennessee, Kentucky, Missouri,
Mississippi, Oklahoma.

April 14, 1937

Mr. Edwin Bjorkman
State Director, Federal Writers' Project
Works Progress Administration
City Hall, Fifth Floor
Asheville, North Carolina

Dear Mr. Bjorkman:

We have received more stories of ex-slaves and are
gratified by the quality and interest of the narratives.
Some of these stories have been accompanied by photographs
of the subjects. We would like to have portraits wherever
they can be secured, but we urge your photographers to
make the studies as simple, natural, and "unposed" as possible. Let the background, cabin or whatnot, be the normal
setting -- in short, just the picture a visitor would expect to find by "dropping in" on one of these old-timers.

Enclosed is a memorandum of Mr. Lomax with suggestions
for simplifying the spelling of certain recurring dialect
words. This does not mean that the interviews should be entirely in "straight English" -- simply, that we want them to
be more readable to those uninitiated in the broadest Negro
speech.

Very truly yours,

George Cronyn
Associate Director
Federal Writers' Project

GWCronyn:MEB

This paragraph was added to the letter to Arkansas.

Mr. Lomax is very eager to get such records as you mention:
Court Records of Sale, Transfer, and Freeing of Slaves, as well
as prices paid.

Negro Dialect Suggestions
(Stories of Ex-Slaves)

Do not write:

Ah for I

Poe for po' (poor)

Hit for it

Tuh for to

Wuz for was

Baid for bed

Daid for dead

Ouh for our

Mah for my

Ovah for over

Othuh for other

Wha for whar (where)

Undah for under

Fuh for for

Yondah for yonder

Moster for marster or massa

Gwainter for gwineter (going to)

Oman for woman

Ifn for iffen (if)

Fiuh or fiah for fire

Uz or uv or o' for of

Poar for poor or po'

J'in for jine

Coase for cose

Utha for other

Yo' for you

Gi' for give

Cot for caught

Kin' for kind

Cose for 'cause

Tho't for thought

WORKS PROGRESS ADMINISTRATION
Federal Writers' Project
1500 Eye St. N.W.
Washington, D. C.

SUPPLEMENTARY INSTRUCTIONS #9-E

To

THE AMERICAN GUIDE MANUAL

FOLKLORE

STORIES FROM EX-SLAVES

Note: In some states it may be possible to locate only
a very few ex-slaves, but an attempt should be
made in every state. Interesting ex-slave data
has recently been reported from Rhode Island, for
instance.

April 22, 1937

STORIES FROM EX-SLAVES

The main purpose of these detailed and homely questions
is to get the Negro interested in talking about the days of slavery.
If he will talk freely, he should be encouraged to say what he pleases
without reference to the questions. It should be remembered that the
Federal Writers' Project is not interested in taking sides on any
question. The worker should not censor any material collected, regard-
less of its nature.

It will not be necessary, indeed it will probably be a mistake, to ask every person all of the questions. Any incidents or facts
he can recall should be written down as nearly as possible just as he
says them, but do not use dialect spelling so complicated that it may
confuse the reader.

A second visit, a few days after the first one, is important,
so that the worker may gather all the worthwhile recollections that the
first talk has aroused.

Questions:

1. Where and when were you born?

2. Give the names of your father and mother. Where did they come
from? Give names of your brothers and sisters. Tell about your life
with them and describe your home and the "quarters." Describe the beds
and where you slept. Do you remember anything about your grandparents
or any stories told you about them?

3. What work did you do in slavery days? Did you ever earn
any money? How? What did you buy with this money?

4. What did you eat and how was it cooked? Any possums?
Rabbits? Fish? What food did you like best? Did the slaves have
their own gardens?

xx

Stories from Ex-slaves -2-

5. What clothing did you wear in hot weather? Cold weather? On Sundays? Any shoes? Describe your wedding clothes.

6. Tell about your master, mistress, their children, the house they lived in, the overseer or driver, poor white neighbors.

7. How many acres in the plantation? How many slaves on it? How and at what time did the overseer wake up the slaves? Did they work hard and late at night? How and for what causes were the slaves punished? Tell what you saw. Tell some of the stories you heard.

8. Was there a jail for slaves? Did you ever see any slaves sold or auctioned off? How did groups of slaves travel? Did you ever see slaves in chains?

9. Did the white folks help you to learn to read and write?

10. Did the slaves have a church on your plantation? Did they read the Bible? Who was your favorite preacher? Your favorite spirituals? Tell about the baptizing; baptizing songs. Funerals and funeral songs.

11. Did the slaves ever run away to the North? Why? What did you hear about patrollers? How did slaves carry news from one plantation to another? Did you hear of trouble between the blacks and whites?

12. What did the slaves do when they went to their quarters after the day's work was done on the plantation? Did they work on Saturday afternoons? What did they do Saturday nights? Sundays? Christmas morning? New Year's Day? Any other holidays? Cornshucking? Cotton Picking? Dances? When some of the white master's family married or died? A wedding or death among the slaves?

13. What games did you play as a child? Can you give the words or sing any of the play songs or ring games of the children? Riddles? Charms? Stories about "Raw Head and Bloody Bones" or other "hants" of ghosts? Stories about animals? What do you think of voodoo? Can you give the words or sing any lullabies? Work songs? Plantation hollers? Can you tell a funny story you have heard or something funny that happened to you? Tell about the ghosts you have seen.

14. When slaves became sick who looked after them? What medicines did the doctors give them? What medicine (herbs, leaves, or roots) did the slaves use for sickness? What charms did they wear and to keep off what diseases?

15. What do you remember about the war that brought your freedom? What happened on the day news came that you were free? What did your master say and do? When the Yankees came what did they do and say?

16. Tell what work you did and how you lived the first year after the war and what you saw or heard about the KuKlux Klan and the Nightriders. Any school then for Negroes? Any land?

17. Whom did you marry? Describe the wedding. How many children and grandchildren have you and what are they doing?

18. What do you think of Abraham Lincoln? Jefferson Davis? Booker Washington? Any other prominent white man or Negro you have known or heard of?

19. Now that slavery is ended what do you think of it? Tell why you joined a church and why you think all people should be religious.

20. Was the overseer "poor white trash"? What were some of his rules?

- - - - - -

The details of the interview should be reported as accurately as possible in the language of the original statements. An example of material collected through one of the interviews with ex-slaves is attached herewith. Although this material was collected before the standard questionnaire had been prepared, it represents an excellent method of reporting an interview. More information might have been obtained however, if a comprehensive questionnaire had been used.

Sample Interview From Georgia

LULA FLANNIGAN
Ex-slave, 78 years.

"Dey says I wuz jes fo' years ole when de war wuz over, but I sho' does member dat day dem Yankee sojers come down de road. Mary and Willie Durham wuz my mammy and pappy, en dey belong ter Marse Spence Durham at Watkinsville in slav'ry times."

"When word cum dat de Yankee sojers wuz on de way, Marse Spence en his sons wuz 'way at de war. Miss Betsey tole my pappy ter take en hide de hosses down in de swamp. My mammy help Miss Betsey sew up de silver in de cotton bed ticks. Dem Yankee sojers nebber did find our whitefolks' hosses and deir silver."

"Miss Marzee, she wuz Marse Spence en Miss Betsey's daughter. She wuz playin' on de pianny when de Yankee sojers come down de road. Two sojers cum in de house en ax her fer ter play er tune dat dey liked. I fergits de name er dey tune. Miss Marzee gits up fum de pianny en she low dat she ain' gwine play no tune for' no Yankee mens. Den de sojers takes her out en set her up on top er de high gate post in front er de big house, en mek her set dar twel de whole regiment pass by. She set dar en cry, but she sho' ain' nebber played no tune for dem Yankee mens!"

"De Yankee sojers tuk all de blankets offen de beds. Dey stole all de meat dey want fum de smokehouse. Dey bash in de top er de syrup barrels en den turn de barrels upside down."

"Marse Spence gave me ter Miss Marzee fer ter be her own maid, but slav'ry time ended fo' I wuz big 'nough ter be much good ter 'er."

Page 2

"Us had lots better times dem days dan now. Whatter dese niggers know 'bout corn shuckin's, en log rollin's, en house raisin's? Marse Spence used ter let his niggers have candy pullin's in syrup mekkin' time, en de way us wud dance in de moonlight wuz sompin' dese niggers nowadays doan know nuffin' 'bout."

"All de white folks love ter see plenty er healthy, strong black chillun comin' long, en dey wuz watchful ter see dat 'omans had good keer when dey chilluns wuz bawned. Dey let dese 'omans do easy, light wuk towards de last 'fo' de chilluns is bawned, en den atterwuds dey doan do nuffin much twel dey is well en strong ergin. Folks tell 'bout some plantations whar de 'omans ud run back home fum de fiel' en hev day baby, en den be back in de fiel' swingin' er hoe fo' night dat same day, but dey woan nuffin lak dat 'round Watkinsville."

"When er scritch owl holler et night us put en iron in de fire quick, en den us turn all de shoes up side down on de flo', en turn de pockets wrong side out on all de close, kaze effen we diden' do dem things quick, sompin' moughty bad wuz sho' ter happen. Mos' en lakly, somebuddy gwint'er be daid in dat house fo' long, if us woan quick 'bout fixin'. Whut us do in summer time, 'bout fire at night fer de scritch owl? Us jes' onkivver de coals in de fire place. Us diden' hev no matches, en us bank de fire wid ashes evvy night all de year 'roun'. Effen de fire go out, kaze some nigger git keerless 'bout it, den somebuddy gotter go off ter de next plantation sometime ter git live coals. Some er de mens could wuk de flints right good, but dat wuz er hard job. Dey jes rub dem flint rocks tergedder right fas' en let de sparks dey makes drap down on er piece er punk wood, en dey gits er fire dat way effen dey is lucky."

"Dem days nobuddy bring er axe in de house on his shoulder. Dat wuz er sho' sign er bad luck. En nebber lay no broom crost de bed. One time er likely pair er black folks git married, en somebuddy give 'em er new broom. De 'oman she proud uv her nice, spankin' new broom en she lay hit on de bed fer de weddin' crowd ter see it, wid de udder things been give 'em. Fo' thee years go by her man wuz beatin' 'er, en not long atter dat she go plum stark crazy. She oughter ter know better'n ter lay dat broom on her bed. It sho' done brung her bad luck. Dey sont her off ter de crazy folks place, en she died dar.

May 3, 1937

Mr. Edwin Bjorkman, State Director
Federal Writers' Project, WPA
City Hall, Fifth Floor
Asheville, North Carolina

                    Subj: Ex-slave Narratives

Dear Mr. Bjorkman:

        I am quoting a memorandum of Mr. Lomax, folklore
editor, regarding the ex-slave stories:

        "Of the five States which have already sent in reminis-
cences of ex-slaves, Tennessee is the only one in which the
workers are asking ex-slaves about their belief in signs, cures,
hoodoo, etc. Also, the workers are requesting the ex-slaves
to tell the stories that were current among the Negroes when
they were growing up. Some of the best copy that has come in
to the office is found in these stories."

        This suggestion, I believe, will add greatly to the
value of the collection now being made.

                        Very truly yours,

                        George Cronyn
                        Associate Director
CC - Mr. W. T. Couch, Asso. Director Federal Writers' Project
        University Press
        Chapel Hill, No. Car.

GWCronyn/a

        SENT TO: No. and So.Carolina; Georgia; Alabama; Louisiana;

                Texas; Arkansas; Kentucky; Missouri; Mississippi;

                Oklahoma; Florida

M E M O R A N D U M

June 9, 1937

TO: STATE DIRECTORS OF THE FEDERAL WRITERS' PROJECT

FROM: Henry G. Alsberg, Director

In connection with the stories of ex-slaves, please send in to this office copies of State, county, or city laws affecting the conduct of slaves, free Negroes, overseers, pat-rollers, or any person or custom affecting the institution of slavery. It will, of course, not be necessary to send more than one copy of the laws that were common throughout the state, although any special law passed by a particular city would constitute worthwhile material.

In addition, we should like to have you collect and send in copies of any laws or accounts of any established customs relating to the admission to your State of bodies of slaves from Africa or other sections, the escape of slaves, etc. Also, we should like to see copies of advertisements of sales of slaves, published offers of rewards for fugitive slaves, copies of transfers of slaves by will or otherwise, records of freeing of slaves, etc. Public records of very particular interest regarding any transaction involving slaves should be photostated and copies furnished to the Washington office.

Furthermore, contemporary accounts of any noteworthy occurrences among the Negroes during slavery days or the Reconstruction period should be copied, if taken from contemporary newspapers. If such records have been published in books, a reference to the source would be sufficient. We have been receiving a large number of extremely interesting stories of ex-slaves. The historic background of the institution of slavery, which should be disclosed with the information we are now requesting, will be very helpful in the execution of the plans we have in mind.

Copies sent to:

Alabama	Georgia	Maryland	North Carolina	Tennessee
Arkansas	Kentucky	Mississippi	Oklahoma	Texas
Florida	Louisiana	Missouri	South Carolina	Virginia
				West Virginia
				Ohio
				Kansas

Notes by an editor on dialect usage in accounts
by interviews with ex-slaves. (To be used in
conjunction with Supplementary Instructions 9E.)

Simplicity in recording the dialect is to be desired in order
to hold the interest and attention of the readers. It seems to
me that readers are repelled by pages sprinkled with misspellings, commas and apostrophes. The value of exact phonetic trans-
cription is, of course, a great one. But few artists attempt
this completely. Thomas Nelson Page was meticulous in his dialect; Joel Chandler Harris less meticulous but in my opinion
even more accurate. But the values they sought are different
from the values that I believe this book of slave narratives
should have. Present day readers are less ready for the over-
stress of phonetic spelling than in the days of local color.
Authors realize this: Julia Peterkin uses a modified Gullah instead of Gonzales' carefully spelled out Gullah. Howard Odum
has questioned the use of goin' for going since the g is seldom
pronounced even by the educated.

Truth to idiom is more important, I believe, than truth to
pronunciation. Erskine Caldwell in his stories of Georgia, Ruth
Suckow in stories of Iowa, and Zora Neale Hurston in stories of
Florida Negroes get a truth to the manner of speaking without
excessive misspellings. In order to make this volume of slave
narratives more appealing and less difficult for the average
reader, I recommend that truth to idiom be paramount, and exact
truth to pronunciation secondary.

I appreciate the fact that many of the writers have recorded sensitively. The writer who wrote "ret" for right is probably as accurate as the one who spelled it "raght." But in a
single publication, not devoted to a study of local speech, the
reader may conceivably be puzzled by different spellings of the
same word. The words "whafolks," "whufolks," "whi'folks," etc.,
can all be heard in the South. But "whitefolks" is easier for
the reader, and the word itself is suggestive of the setting
and the attitude.

Words that definitely have a notably different pronunciation
from the usual should be recorded as heard. More important is
the recording of words with a different local meaning. Most
important, however, are the turns of phrase that have flavor
and vividness. Examples occurring in the copy I read are:

        durin' of de war
        outman my daddy (good, but unnecessarily put into quotes)
        piddled in de fields
        skit of woods
        kinder chillish

There are, of course, questionable words, for which it may
be hard to set up a single standard. Such words are:

        paddyrollers, padrollers, pattyrollers for patrollers
        missis, mistess   for mistress
        marsa, massa, maussa, mastuh   for master
        ter, tuh, teh   for to

I believe   that there should be, for this book, a uniform
word for each of these.

The following list is composed of words which I think
should not be used. These are merely samples of certain faults:

1.	ah	for	I
2.	bawn	for	born
3.	capper	for	caper
4.	com'	for	come
5.	do	for	dough
6.	ebry, ev'ry	for	every
7.	hawd	for	hard
8.	muh	for	my
9.	nakid	for	naked
10.	ole, ol'	for	old
11.	ret, raght	for	right
12.	snaik	for	snake
13.	sowd	for	sword
14.	sto'	for	store
15.	teh	for	tell
16.	twon't	for	twan't
17.	useter, useta	for	used to
18.	uv	for	of
19.	waggin	for	wagon
20.	whi'	for	white
21.	wuz	for	was

I should like to recommend that the stories be told in the language of the ex-slave, without excessive editorializing and "artistic" introductions on the part of the interviewer. The contrast between the directness of the ex-slave speech and the roundabout and at times pompous comments of the interviewer is frequently glaring. Care should be taken lest expressions such as the following creep in: "inflicting wounds from which he never fully recovered" (supposed to be spoken by an ex-slave).

Finally, I should like to recommend that the words darky and nigger and such expressions as "a comical little old black woman" be omitted from the editorial writing. Where the ex-slave himself uses these, they should be retained.

This material sent June 20 to states of: Ala., Ark., Fla., Ga., Ky., La., Md., Miss., Mo., N. C., Ohio, Okla., Tenn., Texas, Va., and S. Car.

M E M O R A N D U M

July 30, 1937.

TO: STATE DIRECTORS OF THE FEDERAL WRITERS' PROJECT

FROM: Henry G. Alsberg, Director

        The following general suggestions are being sent to
all the States where there are ex-slaves still living. They
will not apply in toto to your State as they represent general
conclusions reached after reading the mass of ex-slave material
already submitted. However, they will, I hope, prove helpful
as an indication, along broad lines, of what we want.

GENERAL SUGGESTIONS:

        1. Instead of attempting to interview a large number
of ex-slaves the workers should now concentrate on one or two of
the more interesting and intelligent people, revisiting them,
establishing friendly relations, and drawing them out over a
period of time.

        2. The specific questions suggested to be asked of
the slaves should be only a basis, a beginning. The talk should
run to all subjects, and the interviewer should take care to
sieze upon the information already given, and stories already
told, and from them derive other questions.

        3. The interviewer should take the greatest care not
to influence the point of view of the informant, and not to let
his own opinion on the subject of slavery become obvious. Should
the ex-slave, however, give only one side of the picture, the
interviewer should suggest that there were other circumstances,
and ask questions about them.

        4. We suggest that each state choose one or two of
thier most successful ex-slave interviewers and have them take
down some stories word for word. Some Negro informants are mar-
vellous in their ability to participate in this type of interview.
All stories should be as nearly word-for-word as is possible.

        5. More emphasis should be laid on questions concern-
ing the lives of the individuals since they were freed.

SUGGESTIONS TO INTERVIEWERS:

The interviewer should attempt to weave the following questions naturally into the conversation, in simple language. Many of the interviews show that the workers have simply sprung routine questions out of context, and received routine answers.

1. What did the ex-slaves expect from freedom? Forty acres and a mule? A distribution of the land of their masters' plantation?

2. What did the slaves get after freedom? Were any of the plantations actually divided up? Did their masters give them any money? Were they under any compulsion after the war to remain as servants?

3. What did the slaves do after the war? What did they receive generally? What do they think about the reconstruction period?

4. Did secret organizations such as the Ku Klux Klan exert or attempt to exert any influence over the lives of ex-slaves?

5. Did the ex-slaves ever vote? If so, under what circumstances? Did any of their friends ever hold political office? What do the ex-slaves think of the present restricted suffrage?

6. What have the ex-slaves been doing in the interim between 1864 and 1937? What jobs have they held (in detail)? How are they supported nowadays?

7. What do the ex-slaves think of the younger generation of Negroes and of present conditions?

8. Were there any instances of slave uprisings?

9. Were any of the ex-slaves in your community living in Virginia at the time of the Nat Turner rebellion? Do they remember anything about it?

10. What songs were there of the period?

The above sent to: Alabama, Arkansas, Florida, Ga., Kentucky, La., Md., Mississippi, Mo., N. Car., Okla., S. Car., Tenn., Texas, Virginia, W. Va., Ohio, Kansas, Indiana

M E M O R A N D U M

September 8, 1937

TO: STATE DIRECTORS OF THE FEDERAL WRITERS' PROJECT

FROM: HENRY G. ALSBERG

It would be a good idea if you would ask such of your field workers as are collecting stories from ex-slaves to try to obtain stories given to the ex-slaves by their parents and grandparents. The workers should try to obtain information about family traditions and legends passed down from generation to generation. There should be a wealth of such material available.

We have found that the most reliable way to obtain information about the age of ex-slaves or the time certain events in their lives took place is to ask them to try to recollect some event of importance of known date and to use that as a point of reference. For instance, Virginia had a very famous snow storm called Cox's Snow Storm which is listed in history books by date and which is well remembered by many ex-slaves. In Georgia and Alabama some ex-slaves remember the falling stars of the year 1883. An ex-slave will often remember his life story in relation to such events. Not only does it help the chronological accuracy of ex-slave stories to ask for dated happenings of this kind, but it often serves to show whether the story being told is real or imagined.

Sent the following states:

Alabama	Maryland	Tennessee
Arkansas	Mississippi	Texas
Florida	Missouri	Virginia
Georgia	N. Carolina	West Virginia
Kentucky	Oklahoma	Ohio
Louisiana	S. Carolina	Kansas
		Indiana

TITLES IN THE

SLAVE NARRATIVES SERIES

FROM APPLEWOOD BOOKS

ALABAMA SLAVE NARRATIVES
ISBN 1-55709-010-6 • $14.95
Paperback • 7-1/2" x 9-1/4" • 168 pp

ARKANSAS SLAVE NARRATIVES
ISBN 1-55709-011-4 • $14.95
Paperback • 7-1/2" x 9-1/4" • 172 pp

FLORIDA SLAVE NARRATIVES
ISBN 1-55709-012-2 • $14.95
Paperback • 7-1/2" x 9-1/4" • 168 pp

GEORGIA SLAVE NARRATIVES
ISBN 1-55709-013-0 • $14.95
Paperback • 7-1/2" x 9-1/4" • 172 pp

INDIANA SLAVE NARRATIVES
ISBN 1-55709-014-9 • $14.95
Paperback • 7-1/2" x 9-1/4" • 140 pp

KENTUCKY SLAVE NARRATIVES
ISBN 1-55709-016-5 • $14.95
Paperback • 7-1/2" x 9-1/4" • 136 pp

MARYLAND SLAVE NARRATIVES
ISBN 1-55709-017-3 • $14.95
Paperback • 7-1/2" x 9-1/4" • 88 pp

MISSISSIPPI SLAVE NARRATIVES
ISBN 1-55709-018-1 • $14.95
Paperback • 7-1/2" x 9-1/4" • 184 pp

MISSOURI SLAVE NARRATIVES
ISBN 1-55709-019-X • $14.95
Paperback • 7-1/2" x 9-1/4" • 172 pp

NORTH CAROLINA SLAVE NARRATIVES
ISBN 1-55709-020-3 • $14.95
Paperback • 7-1/2" x 9-1/4" • 168 pp

OHIO SLAVE NARRATIVES
ISBN 1-55709-021-1 • $14.95
Paperback • 7-1/2" x 9-1/4" • 128 pp

OKLAHOMA SLAVE NARRATIVES
ISBN 1-55709-022-X • $14.95
Paperback • 7-1/2" x 9-1/4" • 172 pp

SOUTH CAROLINA SLAVE NARRATIVES
1-55709-023-8 • $14.95
Paperback • 7-1/2" x 9-1/4" • 172 pp

TENNESSEE SLAVE NARRATIVES
ISBN 1-55709-024-6 • $14.95
Paperback • 7-1/2" x 9-1/4" • 92 pp

VIRGINIA SLAVE NARRATIVES
ISBN 1-55709-025-4 • $14.95
Paperback • 7-1/2" x 9-1/4" • 68 pp

* * * * * * * * * * * * * * *

IN THEIR VOICES: SLAVE NARRATIVES
A companion CD of original recordings
made by the Federal Writers' Project.
Former slaves from many states tell
stories, sing long-remembered songs,
and recall the era of American slavery.
This invaluable treasure trove of oral
history, through the power of voices of
those now gone, brings back to life the
people who lived in slavery.
ISBN 1-55709-026-2 • $19.95
Audio CD

* * * * * * * * * * * * * * *

TO ORDER, CALL 800-277-5312 OR
VISIT US ON THE WEB AT WWW.AWB.COM

Milton Keynes UK
Ingram Content Group UK Ltd.
UKHW051608070324
439104UK00013B/998

9 781557 090256